"The Lion, the Witch and

"Best book I have read this decade. Absolutely fabulous
written in 3D just like a film. Got my 8 year old to read,
which is a miracle. Brilliant!"

"Unputdownable."

"My son devoured this book … he's rated it alongside
the Morpurgo books which in his eyes are tip-top."

"It zipped along, and I read it from cover
to cover without stopping."

"This is one of those books that you stumble across and
are so glad you did. I was thrilled to find a book like this
to read to my children. Magic and adventure.
What more could you want?"

"Gripping stuff for children and adults alike.
Full of charm, with a lovely pace."

"This fusion of magic, adventure and excitement
is a breathtaking novel that you can't put down.
I read it in about two days."

"BEST BOOK EVER"

"This book will capture the imagination of adults
and children alike."

"This book captivated my daughter on the first page. She then read the first five chapters without putting it down. No other book has been able to enthral her so completely. I read it to my other children and they loved it, and what's more, so did I."

"This is a real gem of a book which will transport a generation of pre-teens into a wonderfully vivid fantasy world."

"Absolutely loved it ... definitely a page turner ... read it in two sittings."

"I read this cover to cover and couldn't put it down. It transported me into their magical world. My children can't wait for the sequel. They love Tolkien and Potter and we can now add a Loveridge to the list."

"Steven is obviously a very bright and talented author."

"Great!!!!! It was awesome. Everything about it is great. It was so believable and magical. It is one of the best books I have ever read."

"This book is truly amazing. I have been reading it to my children and they love it. They don't want me to stop reading!"

"What a lovely and original book! Full of twists and turns, it keeps even the most imaginative child engaged and enthralled. I'm sure this will be a bestseller - it deserves to be!"

Comments are quoted from reviews on Amazon.

The Palace Library

Steven Loveridge

ISBN: 978-0-9574357-2-8

Leofric Digital
Sandpit
Broadwindsor
Dorset DT8 3RS
United Kingdom

leofricdigital.com

For Edward, Luli and Anouska

The Palace Library
Series

The Palace Library
Guardians of The Scroll

Contents

Followed by sample chapters from the sequel,
Guardians of The Scroll

1. The Palace Library

Grace knew she wasn't allowed in the Long Gallery. She also knew she would be late for tea. But it looked far too much fun. The room was vast, with old tapestries lining the walls. Most of all, the floors were made for running and sliding. Grace sped along the old carpets, then she skidded along the floorboards between them.

At the end of the room, Grace was surfing at high speed along the last piece of polished floor and tripped on the edge of the carpet. She fell on her face with a thud and tried not to cry out in case she was heard. Then she saw the dog. Huge, like a giant hairy greyhound and at least as tall as Grace, it seemed to be snarling. She did the only sensible thing she could think of. She shut her eyes tight, held her head in her hands, and hoped it would go away.

What seemed like an age later, she opened one eye and saw the dog was just a picture on a tapestry, not a real dog at all. "Silly me! You can't be frightened of a picture," said Grace to herself, finding her own voice reassuring, even though she did not really feel it. She looked at the tapestry again. The dog was actually a deerhound, and seemed much happier than the snarling vision Grace thought she had seen. She stood up and gently touched the woven fabric of the tapestry to check, stroking the dog's shoulder as if it was real. The picture leapt to life. The dog emerged from the tapestry, wriggled and turned on its back with a gentle whine, as if it wanted to be stroked more.

This was quite enough for Grace. She leapt up, ran to the side of the Long Gallery and stood with her back to the wall, breathing very quickly and unsteadily. This time she kept her eyes open. Once again, the tapestry became quite normal, but the picture had changed. The dog was now lying on its front, looking at her.

Grace slowly pushed herself along the wall, trying not to be noticed. It was then that she discovered the door. She could have sworn the door had not been there before. Grace was only eight years old - nearly nine, she told people - so she really noticed this door. It was exactly the right size for her and had a round stone arch over it with a zigzag pattern. Adults would have had to bend nearly double to get through, so maybe it was just a cupboard. But it didn't look like a cupboard and it looked very old. It was made of heavy dark wood and it fascinated her.

All Grace's instincts told her to run away from the scary tapestry, but the door seemed to say to her: "Come on. Try me."

She drew in a big breath, shut her eyes tight and counted to 10. Opening her eyes again the tapestry still seemed normal, so she decided to turn the handle on the door and try pushing it. It seemed locked. She tried again without it working. It still wouldn't move. Then, she gave it a big shove and it opened so quickly that Grace slipped and fell on her face. After a pause, there was a thump and then another thump and then three more in quick succession. Thump... thump... thump! This time Grace had kept her eyes open. What she saw was quite unexpected. She was looking down at the floor of a huge library from the very top of a bookshelf. This was no ordinary bookshelf. It was a very tall bookshelf, and the door had opened directly onto it. The thumps were books that had fallen off and were lying on the floor beneath her. They looked miles away. As Grace looked around the room, she saw it was full of thousands and thousands of old books. The odd thing was that it was full of sunlight. Yet Grace knew that outside it was grey and raining. Terrified, whilst holding onto the shelf and trying not to fall, she noticed a very old man with a white beard, wearing a magnificent blue tailcoat covered in gold swirly brocade.

"Hello there," the man said cheerfully, in a slightly bumbling way. "I wasn't expecting you. No one's used that door for years. Hold on and I'll find you a ladder."

Grace couldn't move. Her fingers gripped the shelf so hard that her knuckles went white. The man pushed a huge ladder on wheels towards her. It was like a very smart wooden fire engine ladder, but it was so tall that the top swayed madly from side to side. She thought it might hit her.

This was all too much for Grace. She picked herself up and quickly ran back down the Long Gallery the way she had come. Just before she left the room, she turned and everything seemed normal. She thought she would just check on the weather outside again, so she stood on tiptoes to see out. Sure enough, the rain was battering on the windowpanes.

Then the man with the white beard poked his head through the tiny door and looked at her. Towering over him was the dog. "There's no need to run away. I've put the ladder up now. Do come back."

Grace saw the sun shining through the door and couldn't understand it, so she ran from the corridor as fast as she could. The best thing to do would be to tell her cousins Harry and Eleanor. They could explore together and maybe Harry, who was 12 and the oldest of the three, would have an explanation.

2. Chocolate Cake

The problem with The Palace Library is that no one knows where it is. In fact, very few people know that it even exists. Of the very few people who know it exists, very few know how to find it. Grace had discovered it and was longing to share her news and find out more.

Unfortunately, before she could do that, Horrible Hair Bun found her and shouted at her. The children used this name for the housekeeper when they knew she couldn't hear. Her grey hair was always tied up in a very tight bun at the back of her head. It had wispy bits sticking out, which matched the curly bits of hair on her chin. The children just wished they could pluck them out, especially when she kissed them goodnight and they tickled and prickled.

Grace was late for tea. She was made to sit in silence and watch Eleanor and Harry eat their chocolate pudding while she was only allowed dry spaghetti without sauce.

Grace could hardly contain herself, but whenever she tried

to talk, Horrible Hair Bun just shouted, "Quiet."

Eventually, just before bedtime, Grace explained to Harry and Eleanor what had happened.

Harry was rather abrupt. "Don't be silly Grace. You're making it up. There's no such thing as a magic room with magic dogs. Anyway, I've been in Great Uncle Jasper's library. It's full of books for sure, but it's not that big." Then he went off to his own bedroom.

Eleanor looked at Harry as he left and thought he was being rather mean. It wasn't really like him. She realised that they had ignored Grace all day. Eleanor saw a lot of her brother Harry, but not so much of her cousin. It was their chance to catch up and play since they were all together for the summer holidays at Great Uncle Jasper's house. And they ought to be nicer to Grace. She'd been an orphan since her parents had died in a car crash several years earlier. Being together was the whole point of coming to their uncle's house after all. They could get together and enjoy being outside in the vast gardens and grounds, especially since Harry and Eleanor's house only had a tiny back yard.

The problem was that there was so much rain that August, everyone was miserable. They couldn't go outside. Water was seeping in through the window frames and Horrible Hair Bun had placed buckets to catch drops coming through the ceiling. Everyone was bored and there was nothing to do but stay inside.

Grace had been very fed up earlier that day. Harry and Eleanor weren't being deliberately mean to her, but it felt as if they were. They were ignoring her and playing without her. That was when Grace had begun to explore different parts of the house on her own. It was big enough.

Eleanor tried to make Grace feel better, but even she added, "Magic isn't real, Grace. Why not go to bed now and maybe you can show us the big room in the morning."

Grace began to wonder if she had just imagined it after all. Never mind. She would check tomorrow - but when the others were not looking, so that she could be sure.

The next afternoon, Grace told Harry and Eleanor that she was fed up with the game they were playing and she slipped away. They both seemed to have forgotten about the night before anyway. Feeling very nervous, Grace went back to the Long Gallery and found the door again. She looked at the tapestry outside the door and thought it was strange that the dog woven into the pattern seemed to be sleeping, and was not snarling or smiling. This time she certainly wasn't going to touch it. Grace hesitated at the door, and then pushed it.

The door opened easily enough this time and she found the funny ladder she had seen swaying the previous day, but now it was fixed to the top of the bookshelf. The steps were steep, made of highly polished wood with a brass handrail on one side. Grace realised it would have been more sensible to have gone down backwards, but then she might have missed everything there was to see. So she went down very gingerly, step by step, and enjoyed looking at the sun shining on all the leather bound books. There were 29 steps in all. Grace counted them out loud as she went. At the bottom the cheerful man in the blue tailcoat and white beard appeared from nowhere and said, "Hello. I'm so glad you have come back. Welcome to The Palace Library. It's time for tea, I think. Shall we have chocolate cake?"

Since Grace had missed her chocolate pudding the day before, she said, "Oh yes please." Suddenly the man and The Library did not seem so scary at all.

"Come on then. The cookery section is around the next corner."

"Do we need a recipe to bake it?"

"Not exactly, Grace," said the old man. "This is a library after all, not a kitchen, but everything is in the books."

Grace wondered how he knew her name, but found that grown-ups often knew her name without asking.

They walked around the corner to a shelf of books that were very nearly as tall as Grace. "Here we are," said the old man. "*Best Baking*. I'll need your help, please." The book was rather large - over four feet high and two feet wide, and they struggled to place it on the table. "Page 36 if I remember rightly, but it's a long time since I've had this cake. I don't get much company anymore."

He opened the book and there was a huge picture of a fantastic looking cake with gorgeous icing. It was covered in chocolate buttons. The extraordinary thing was that as Grace looked at the picture, it stopped being a picture and turned slowly into a real cake. "I think this one must be a quick-bake recipe," said the old man with a chuckle. "Let's tuck in."

As they ate the cake, the man asked Grace about her friends and said she ought to bring them back to tea another day. She finally plucked up the courage to ask him his name. "Most people just call me the Librarian, but perhaps you could call me Edgar. They used to call me Edgar once and I rather liked it."

16

"Is that Mr Edgar then?" Grace asked politely. "I am always being told I should call grown-ups Mr or Mrs something."

"No," said the old man. "Just Edgar. I'd prefer it that way. Now run along or you'll be late for your proper tea."

Just as Grace got to the ninth step on the ladder, Edgar called to her. "Borrow this book. You might enjoy it. Be sure to bring your friends back and tell me whether you liked it."

"Thank you," said Grace. She looked at the cover and saw it said *The Owl and the Pussy Cat*. "It's one of my favourites."

"Ah yes, but the pictures in this one are particularly good," said Edgar with a twinkle in his eye. "Just mind you keep it closed at night. It does have a tendency to leak. Goodbye."

Grace had never heard of a book leaking before.

3. The Leaking Book

Grace was sent to bed early by Horrible Hair Bun. Try as she might, Grace was unable to eat her tea after all the delicious chocolate cake in The Palace Library. Even now, no one believed her about her discovery of the magical library. So when Horrible Hair Bun frogmarched her to the bedroom and turned the key in the door, she settled into bed, somewhat sad and lonely. Being an orphan Grace was rather too used to being sad and lonely. She wished she could remember her parents better. At least she was excited about reading the book that Edgar the Librarian had lent her. She fell asleep with it, and it lay open on the bed beside her all night.

The next morning, the shimmer of light breaking through badly drawn curtains woke Eleanor. "At last," she said to herself, seeing the bright sunlight, "we can go and play outside and explore the gardens." She knew it was very early, but she wanted to find Grace and tell her the good news. She had missed Grace the night before and felt guilty about not being kinder to her. The bad weather really had made them all grumpy.

The floorboards in the old house squeaked. Along the corridor towards Grace's room, Eleanor crept and nervously stretched her toes to remembered places on the floor in a well-practised routine. A week in the old house ensured the journey was silent so that she did not wake up any adults. She quietly turned the key in the lock outside Grace's room. Horrible Hair Bun had left the key in the door. She jumped on Grace's bed and said, "Wake up! Wake up! It's sunny at last. Let's go outside and play."

Grace was pretty sleepy, but she soon woke up. Soon enough to hear Eleanor's next words properly: "Yuck, Grace. You've wet your bed."

Grace was cross at that. She never wet her bed. But she had an answer: "Don't be silly, Eleanor. The book has leaked. I was reading it and left it open when I fell asleep."

Eleanor was nearly a year and a half older than Grace and reckoned herself to be considerably wiser, so she was able to say with a certain authority that, "Books most certainly don't leak, Grace. You're the one being silly."

Grace wasn't going to let her get away with that, so she held the book up above the blankets "This one leaks. The Librarian told me it might, but I don't know what to do about all the water."

Eleanor looked in astonishment at the page of the book that Grace was holding up. She could read the words, "The Owl and the Pussy Cat went to sea in a beautiful pea green boat," but what amazed her was the way the pictures moved, not like a television programme or like a cartoon, but in a way that made you think you were really at sea with the Owl and the Pussy Cat. Then she realised what Grace meant. The pages were dripping water on the bed. The girls looked at each other and giggled.

Then Eleanor looked seriously at Grace. In a very nice, civilised and grown up way, she said, "I'm sorry I didn't believe you about The Palace Library, Grace. I should have known you wouldn't lie." Then the girls giggled again and Eleanor jumped under the covers with Grace. They read the whole of Edward Lear's famous poem with all the pictures again, even though the bed sheets were a bit damp.

When they had finished, Eleanor said to Grace, "What on earth are we are going to say to Horrible Hair Bun about the sheets? She's so strict and she'll never believe us about the book leaking. I don't want you to be in any more trouble."

They were worried and sat up to think about it, closing the pale yellow cover of the book as they did so. With the cover shut, the book began to draw all the water out of the sheets. It was like someone sucking up a drink with a straw and using blotting paper all at the same time. Moments later, the sheets were completely dry. The girls looked at each other in awe and then giggled again.

Grace thought for a moment: "Shall we go and give the book back to the Librarian and tell him what fun it was? Maybe he'll lend us another one if we show him we can look after it?"

Then Eleanor added, "Shall we ask Harry to come too?"

4. The Great West Door

The girls decided that if they tried to get dressed, they would make too much noise. They also thought that if they went to wake Harry, they would make even more noise and anyway, Grace still thought he would be mean to her. So they put on their dressing gowns and crept along the corridors avoiding as many of the squeaking floorboards as they could.

Grace stopped suddenly and put her hand on Eleanor's shoulder.

"What is it?" Eleanor whispered.

"I think we should get Harry after all," Grace replied.

"Are you sure?" replied Eleanor, but she smiled thinking it was the right decision.

"Yes. If he doesn't believe me then that's too bad, but it would be a pity not to tell him where we're going."

When they turned to go back the way they had come, they were less cautious about the floorboards and several squeaked. They seemed extra loud passing Horrible Hair Bun's room, but they stood still and listened carefully holding their breath. Nothing. So they turned the corner to Harry's room.

Harry's door was wide open with the lights blazing. It was a mess. It was as if Harry had dressed very quickly and left everything else on the floor. Now if it had been at home, Eleanor would not have been surprised. Her brother's room was a mess all the time there, but here at Great Uncle Jasper's house, it was different. Horrible Hair Bun was so strict that they kept all their rooms pristine.

The girls walked into the room and looked around.

"Where is he?" asked Eleanor. "Where's he gone?"

The deep voice that replied made them jump and they turned round to face Great Uncle Jasper and both felt slightly sheepish. Horrible Hair Bun stood just behind him, frowning as usual, but looking subdued and strained.

"I had to send him out to The Palace Library," said their Great Uncle quietly.

"Do you want me to get them dressed?" asked the housekeeper, interrupting.

"No. There will be no time. Edgar will have to see to that," he said sharply and without explanation. Great Uncle Jasper turned to her. "Perhaps you could prepare my breakfast. I will speak to the girls alone." It was a dismissal and the girls looked on in awe, as they had never seen Horrible Hair Bun receiving orders before.

"Come with me girls. We will need to talk as we go." It was the gentle voice they knew again. Great Uncle Jasper put his hands out. They didn't know him that well and normally he was a distant figure, but it was a comforting gesture and they each took one of his hands as they walked.

"I need to send you after Harry. I have sent him out to The Library on an important journey. Time is short, so he has gone ahead. He will need your help."

"Why did you say 'out' to The Library again? Isn't it in your house? Doesn't Edgar work for you?" asked Grace.

"You are very sharp to notice that, Grace; but no, The Palace Library isn't in this house, although it may appear so to you. The Palace Library is so well hidden that even the few people who know about it sometimes have trouble finding it. It doesn't have any doors in the conventional sense. The doors into The Library are quite different to our normal understanding. They may not really even exist in our world at all. The Library has a way of summoning people to it. People like you and Eleanor and Harry.

"I am one of the lucky ones who know about The Library. But even I can't always find it. The Library finds me. It can reach through history to find those who, like you, can help in a crisis. I am one of a council called The Witan that it reaches out to."

"You make it sound like a person," said Eleanor. She was a little out of breath. Great Uncle Jasper was a tall man with big strides and they were struggling to keep up.

"Not a person really, but something with a personality anyway."

Suddenly, they were there. They stopped by the small door in the Long Gallery. Great Uncle Jasper squatted down to look at them at eye level and spoke to them as equals. "You know where to go from here, Grace. I sent for Harry earlier and was about to send for both of you before I found you in Harry's room. There is no time to talk or to tell you more. Edgar will give you what you need. Good luck."

With that, he gave them each a kiss on their cheeks and strode back to the end of the room. Grace and Eleanor felt lonely and bereft as he left. There were too many unanswered questions. With the hands that had been holding his, they found each other's hands and as he left the corridor, he turned and said, "Trust each other, as friends and families should." Then he smiled. "When you see Harry, I don't think he'll have any doubts about a magical library any longer."

Both girls hesitated before going through the door. Grace looked at the tapestry on the wall and said to Eleanor, "This picture has changed again. The dog was sleeping last time I was here, and growling the time before that."

"She's looking impatient here isn't she?" said Eleanor. "It's as if she's been pacing up and down waiting for something or someone."

"Maybe she's waiting for us," said Grace

"She's a very beautiful dog," added Eleanor, putting off the scary moment when they would open the door.

"How do you know the dog's a girl?" asked Grace.

"I just know," replied Eleanor mysteriously. "And stop holding my hand so tightly." But Grace noticed she didn't let go or release her own tight grip. They were both shivering, even though it wasn't cold. Then they opened the door.

This time The Library was dark. It looked as if it was dusk outside and there was a terrible storm raging. There was a domed roof high above them with a lantern window. Lightning burst with rolls of thunder sounding almost immediately. The light threw strange shadows around the room and the books.

The girls were more than a little frightened, especially

when they turned around and saw the sun shining through the windows of the long corridor. Grace and Eleanor looked at each other and paused. Grace took a deep breath, let go of Eleanor's hand and said, "Follow me." They climbed down the ladder - counting all 29 steps carefully. At the bottom of the stairs, they found Edgar the Librarian. He was waiting for them.

"Good morning, good morning," he said fiddling with his hands impatiently, "if it is morning. It's so hard to tell sometimes. How nice to meet you, Eleanor." It was immediately clear to Grace that he was a lot more serious than the previous day, even though he was still terribly polite. "I didn't know whether you would be here at all, but I thought I'd wait anyway. The thing is I'm just a little worried about Harry. He seems to have vanished and I think he has gone out of another door."

Grace wondered whether she should be cross with Harry for not believing her, but for now she was just worried about him. There was too much to take in.

Edgar continued, "Perhaps it was foolish of me to let him go wandering around on his own. It has been such a long time since The Library allowed two doors to be opened at once; I had forgotten it might be a problem."

"What do you mean 'The Library allowed'? Don't you mean *you* allowed?'" asked Eleanor, echoing Grace's question to Great Uncle Jasper.

"Oh no, I mean The Library," said Edgar, without offering more of an explanation. "I'm just the Librarian. But now you're here and you should be able to help. You can go after Harry. I'm sure he's gone through the Great West Door."

"But why couldn't you go after him?" asked Grace. "I know

he's older than us, but he's still not even a teenager?"

"I'm not allowed out of The Palace Library. When The Witan and the late King gave me the position, I knew that would be the case. It's a great burden sometimes, but it is my duty. Never mind. I have plenty to read. You're here now. We should still have enough time before the door closes again, I hope."

Eleanor had been learning about history at school, so she brightly asked: "The late King? Do you mean George VI, the Queen's father? We've learnt about him."

"No, no," said Edgar distractedly. "Not him. Long before his reign… but there's no time to tell you now. We must get you ready. I've been thinking about books that might help you on your journey. Then perhaps you can take one for Harry too. He'll need a different sort of book to you two girls I think."

"Why do we need books to help us find Harry?" Eleanor asked.

"Not to find him. I hope you won't have any problem finding Harry. You'll need books to get you ready for going through the door and to help you all when you get there. The Library only allows two doors to be open at the same time at a time of need and it has a way of calling the people who might be able to help. That's clearly why you're all here, but of course you don't know that yet."

"Yes we do," said Eleanor. "Great Uncle Jasper told us. He sent us. Harry too."

Edgar looked at them strangely and with a little more respect. "Did he now? That would explain a lot. I wish he'd told me too, but perhaps there wasn't time. It's funny. I spend so long with nothing to do but read, and then everything happens at once."

Suddenly both girls jumped as a great bell tolled. It filled the room with sound, but at the same time seemed very distant, before slowly fading away. Just before it finally faded, the same bell rang once more and the girls jumped again.

Edgar looked alert. "We must hurry before the bells finish ringing. Quickly now!"

In spite of what he said, Edgar didn't move. "I need to call Sophie."

"Who's Sophie?" the girls asked together.

"Sophie will accompany you," replied Edgar. "She is my companion here and she'll be your companion on your journey. Long ago, Sophie was the gift of a great Queen, who, like you," continued Edgar, turning towards the elder of the girls, "was called Eleanor. Sophie has great empathy, but be warned, although she'll protect you and love you, she won't suffer fools."

"What's empa-, empa-? Oh you know what I mean," asked Grace.

"Empathy means she will know what you think and feel, often before you know it yourself. And you," said Edgar, this time turning to Grace, "have already met her."

"Have I?"

Edgar did not reply. Instead he drew a slender silver whistle from inside his jacket and blew it. The girls heard nothing but just stared. A moment later, silently and as if by magic, Sophie was standing at Edgar's side and Grace understood. Even though she understood, she took a step back fearfully. For Sophie was the dog from the carpet and she appeared to be snarling.

But Eleanor, who had a real fondness for animals, was enchanted. She realised that Sophie was smiling, even though most dogs do not smile. Edgar leant down to pat the neck of the elegant deerhound. "Eleanor and Grace, don't be afraid. Come and meet Sophie." They stepped forward, waiting to be introduced, since they knew you must always be introduced to dogs first. As Grace and Eleanor were only just taller than the deerhound, Sophie licked their noses and smiled again and they both cuddled her and hugged her neck.

"Remember this girls. Sophie is not a pet. Although she doesn't speak, you must regard her as your equal, for she is a royal hunting dog and has a lineage as great as, or greater than many of the kings in the world. She will be a comfort to you."

Just then the bell rang again and the girls jumped, but Sophie stood firm. Edgar was right. She was a comfort already.

Edgar was less of a comfort as he said, "Now we must go and find your books and get you equipped. If that bell stops ringing before you go through the Great West Door, the door may vanish and Harry will be on his own. Who knows if you will ever see him again?"

5. Three Magical Books

"Follow me," said Edgar the Librarian to Grace and Eleanor, far too calmly for their liking after his last statement. "I'm going to give you each a book to take with you. Use them wisely and learn from them. I'll give you each gifts to help as well. They will be yours to use where you go, but you must bring them back to The Library. The Library won't allow you to take them home."

"First, we must go to the astronomy section. As you would expect, it is right at the top, near the sky. Come. There's a quicker way than up the ladder you came in on." Edgar slipped behind the book stacks and they found themselves on a circular stone staircase. "Don't worry. There are only 127 steps!"

Eleanor and Grace looked at each other, but before they had time to think about what a long way it was, Edgar turned and said: "Come on. Sophie will wait here." Then the bell tolled again and they jumped to follow him.

The steps did not seem to bother Edgar, but both girls were quite out of breath by the time they arrived at the top. They found themselves in a gallery, a little like the one underneath the dome at St Paul's Cathedral in London, but this one was lined with books.

Half way around, Edgar paused and pulled out a large book from a shelf at the bottom. He struggled with it and they had to stop him from falling over backwards with it. It was very nearly as big as the book with the chocolate cake.

Once the book was on a table, he opened it. Both girls gasped. On the pages were maps of the skies. Drawn beautifully, they were similar to star maps the girls had seen at home. Better than this though, the stars shot out of the pages like shooting stars and clung onto the dome, which now glowed dark blue. There, the stars glimmered and glittered. It was like looking directly up at the night sky. In fact the only way you could tell that it was not the night sky was that the lightning through the lantern window was still throwing patterns across the bookshelves and the inside of the dome.

"Wow!" Grace cried out.

"This is for you, Grace," said Edgar. "It seems that you're an explorer and so this book will help you navigate. With the other gift I'll give you, you can use the stars and the Sun to find your way."

"Thank you," stammered Grace, "but how will I carry it?"

"I'll make you the pocket version," answered Edgar. "Will you just open that drawer there, please?" He pointed to a deep wide drawer at about eye height for Grace. It was between bookshelves and she opened it. Edgar struggled with the book again and put it inside before locking the drawer with a golden key from his pocket and saying, "Move across to the other side of the dome now please."

At the other side of the dome, Edgar found another much smaller drawer and opened it with the same golden key. When Grace opened the drawer, she found a much smaller copy of the same book. "It's such a handy system for taking books with you when you're travelling. I'm afraid you'll find it's still quite heavy, but much more manageable. You look after it now, Grace. We're going to take the quick way down."

With that, Edgar slipped behind the book stack into a tiny space. "There's just room for three!"

Just as soon as they stood on it, Edgar released a brass lever at the side and said, "Hold on!" It was like the sensation of jumping off a tall diving board into a swimming pool, but it lasted much longer. The girls were glad they had not eaten breakfast as they felt as if their stomachs were left behind them. Moments later, the platform bounced several times, rather like landing on a bouncy castle, before staying still.

"That was fun," said Grace trying to disguise her nerves and the fact that she felt a little sick. "I wish we could do it again."

"No time I'm afraid," replied Edgar, adding, "personally, I try to take the steps if I have the time!"

As they all stepped off the platform, the girls realised they were in a quite different part of The Library. The air was colder and much of the glamorous panelling in the main part gave way to stone walls.

"It's down here in the basement that we've come to find your gift, Eleanor," explained Edgar.

They walked along the corridor and passed several metal grates, locked with large padlocks. They could have been prison cells, but behind each one the girls could see row upon row of books lit by a strange greenish light. Each 'cell' went on so far that they could not see the end.

Eleanor was more than a little in awe of where they were and asked, "Are these secret books Edgar? Is that why they're locked up?"

Edgar stopped and turned to her, apparently now taking his time. "No these aren't secret books. These books are locked up because they're dangerous. Just here," he said, turning to one passage, "is the section on crocodiles. Now we wouldn't want them escaping would we?" He sighed, bumbling, almost forgetting his haste. "It's the arachnid section I really don't like."

"Arachnids?" asked Eleanor.

"Spiders," said Edgar.

"Yuck!"

"The gates just there are never cleaned just in case we muddle the real spiders and the magical spiders. It's such a mess. I'll show you one day." Then the bell tolled again reminding them of the need for more haste. "Come on. Less chat!"

Grace and Eleanor both wished Sophie was with them, wondering whether they were more frightened of crocodiles or spiders.

Edgar had not moved though and was suddenly serious. "It's time I explained something to you both and it's something that you must explain to Harry. There are no secret books in The Palace Library. The Library represents both the freedom of knowledge and the memories and justice of England. That is why The Witan set it up and wanted it protected. It's my duty to look after it. The fact that The Library often remains hidden is due to the very fact that sometimes people want the knowledge in The Library to be hidden and want to suppress freedom. It is The Library's paradox, but it is always open to anyone who truly seeks knowledge."

"What's a para-, para-, para-... you know?" asked Grace.

"It's something that appears to be contradictory, but turns out not to be and yet at the same time is difficult to understand. You probably think it's a bit strange that The Library is hidden but not secret. That is a paradox."

"OK," said Eleanor as cheerfully as the circumstances allowed, wanting to make it clear to Grace that she understood, although she did not quite. Grace remained silent, unconvinced either by the explanation or by Eleanor's confident understanding.

"Come on now," said Edgar. "We must get you your book. It's in the next book stack on the left."

Eleanor's book was a quite different colour and size. It would not need shrinking like the astronomy book and it was bound in beautiful burgundy coloured leather, with pictures of thistles embossed in gold on the cover.

"We'll open this one upstairs," said Edgar, mysteriously.

At the top of a short flight of stairs, they nearly tripped over Sophie, who was waiting for them, wise enough to know they would appear from the basement.

When Edgar opened Eleanor's book, she found it was full of pictures of plants with tiny writing next to them, which even she struggled to read with her good eyesight. In a way, Eleanor was a little disappointed with the book, as it looked just like a 'normal' book, although the pictures were very beautifully drawn.

She tried not to look too disappointed when she asked Edgar what the book was about. "It is about healing. You must study it well."

"Why was it locked up with the dangerous books then?" she asked.

"What can heal can also poison. With the knowledge in this book, you can cure many diseases. But wrongly used or used with evil intent, this knowledge can also kill. That is why it's dangerous. Take it now."

Eleanor took the book gingerly and far from being disappointed, she became quite worried about what she realised was a responsibility. Sophie seemed to sense her anxiety and the deerhound put a paw on her shoulder and licked her face. Eleanor smiled.

Edgar crossed the room to a great wooden cabinet and brought out two items.

To Eleanor, he gave a short dagger in its own scabbard. "This is for your protection. The dagger can also be used to cut plants. Do not try to fight with it, unless absolutely necessary. Look to Harry to be your warrior and champion if needed."

The dagger was mounted on a leather girdle, which Eleanor buckled around her waist. As she did so, she noticed an engraving of a tiny dragon on the buckle. She began to pull the dagger from its case and noticed a strange dim greenish glow, but Edgar stopped her, saying, "You do not need weapons in The Palace Library."

To Grace he gave a golden pocket watch on a long gold chain. He put it over her neck and showed her how to open one side to tell the time. The other side was a compass. "With the watch and the compass and your book, you can navigate.

Don't forget to wind the watch every day."

As he finished, a different bell began to toll with long steady strokes and Edgar looked alarmed. "We must hurry! That is the final bell for Compline."

Eleanor and Grace looked at each other quizzically, wondering which one of them was going to ask what Compline was, but fortunately Edgar continued, "It is the last church service of the day and is calling the great gathering of the Court to the chapel. These bells are not ringing in The Library, but we can hear them through the Great West Door. Once the bell stops ringing, the door will be locked and you will not be able to reach Harry. Come! We have no more than five minutes."

Edgar did not appear to be moving that quickly, but the girls had to run to keep up with him and Sophie followed at Eleanor's heels. As they went he pulled some books from the shelves. Grace saw the title on one said *Plantagenet Fashion*. Another seemed very plain and thin.

They turned a corner and walked up to the Great West Door. Unlike the small door they had used to enter The Library, this was a pair of double doors which a giant could walk through. There was a smaller door set into the left hand one, a wicket gate. When they got there, Edgar turned the pages of the first book and seemed to flick things off them towards the girls. They suddenly realised their clothes had changed. They were no longer in their nighties. They were in deep purple gowns and long cloaks made of fur, quite unlike anything they had seen outside of history books at school.

"Somehow, I didn't think you'd look quite right in your night-clothes," chuckled Edgar. Then he added seriously, "You need to remember this. This door is not a door into The

Library. It is a door out of The Library to somewhere else. You may need to find another way back into The Library. You must go and find Master John and ask for the Queen's help. Now! Hurry! Go and help Harry."

"But where are we going?" said the girls in unison.

"Haven't I told you?" replied Edgar with a frown. "How very careless of me. It's not so much a matter of where as when."

"When?" asked the girls, finding this all quite hard to follow. Even wrapped up in their furs, they were both starting to shiver with cold and anxiety.

"Yes, *when*. If I'm not mistaken, January 1164, for this is the Great West Door of Clarendon Palace and the most important men in the kingdom are gathered there."

As Edgar spoke, the rhythm of the bells changed and the girls asked more and more questions.

"Silence!" said Edgar. "The Library has chosen you, so you must go and join Harry. There is no more time for questions. Give Harry this book. It will give him wisdom at a time of need and perhaps when he least expects it, but warn him it will be cryptic. His clothes will do. At least he was not in pyjamas!"

With that, the final stroke of the bell began to fade and Edgar held open the small wicket gate set into the main doors. A blast of much colder air hit them. Sophie nudged both girls into a Great Hall. Then when the girls looked around through the open gate, they could not see The Library, but only the rain coming down on the sodden grass of a dark winter night at Clarendon Palace in January 1164.

They felt very lonely, but Sophie seemed to know where she was going. They followed her.

6. Harry's Story

The Great Hall had a vast wooden roof. The hall was crowded and it was probably a good thing that no one seemed to pay them any attention. Sophie led the girls around the edge of the hall and out of a side door. The girls noticed they were now under some sort of gallery. A roof above their head protected them from the worst of the weather, but the side was open to the elements and they both felt the cold, so they pulled their fur cloaks around them. Rain dripped off the edge of the roof and blew into their faces.

Sophie paused at the corner before putting her nose in the air and sniffing. She smiled, just like the first time Grace had met her, although back then she had mistaken it for a snarl. Then she moved off and the girls were both hard put to keep up with her. Sophie pushed at a door and went through it. There was a warm glow coming from the room inside and a delicious smell of roasting meat.

In the room, in front of a huge fire, there was a whole hog

roasting on a spit. A large man and a short fat woman stood with their backs to them. The man was wearing a long green coat with leather trousers and braid on his sleeves. The woman was obviously a cook and was tending to the meat. Sophie came up behind the man and put her nose into his side. He was clearly used to dogs as he put his hand down to stroke her nose and carried on his conversation. Sophie was a bit more insistent before he turned around to look.

Then he turned and she put her feet up and licked his face, really smiling again, in that funny way that only special dogs do. That surprised the man a lot and he said sharply, "Get down now," before he took more notice and said with surprise, "Sophie! Is that you? How did you come to be here? You look so well and so healthy. The Queen had said we were unlikely to see you again."

At that, Sophie dropped down and went behind the girls and pushed them towards the man, wagging her tail. They were both terrified, but he looked down at them and said, "So who are you? Sophie seems to know you so I guess you can't be all bad."

At that moment, there was a loud shout. The cook noticed them and said, "Master John. You're bad enough bringing a dog into my kitchen, but you know I won't have children here! Remove them at once!" The girls stared at her and their eyes opened wide at what they saw. "Now!" shouted the woman, waving a long iron ladle at them.

The man shooed them out the kitchen into the cloister. "Mistress Comely, the cook, has a wicked mouth but a heart of gold. Don't you worry about her." The man was like a giant, but gentle and made the girls feel a little more comfortable and at ease. Then they caught each other's eye. They were nervous and they giggled.

The man looked at them a little strangely. "Now what is that all about? The girls glanced at each other knowingly and Grace whispered to Eleanor, "You tell him. You're older."

So Eleanor did, rather shyly, but smiling. "It's just that she looks exactly like Horrible Hair Bun, but half the height and as if she'd been blown up with a bicycle pump. And they've both got funny little hairs growing on their face." They giggled again.

The man looked at them carefully. "You're mighty cheeky for ones so young." The girls looked crestfallen, as if a joke and a shared confidence had gone badly wrong, but he continued, "I know nothing about Mistress Hair Bun, nor what a bicycle pump is. But Mistress Comely has a heart of gold, however bad her temper seems, and her cooking is divine." It might have been a telling off, but suddenly he smiled. He pointed to his beard, and added, "There are a fair few funny hairs on my face too, but you're right about one thing; there a great many things I'd think of doing before I wanted to kiss Mistress Comely with her prickly hairs!"

He roared at the joke and they laughed together, the girls relieved that they seemed to have found a friend. Then Eleanor looked a little more serious and asked, "We're looking for Master John. And we're also looking for Harry. Do you know them?"

Now to a grown-up, these questions might have seemed strange, especially since the girls had just come through a magical library and stepped back in time over 800 years, but to Eleanor it seemed to be the most natural question in the world.

"You seem to be in luck now. I guess that's thanks to Sophie. I am Master John and you must be Eleanor and Grace. Wait a moment now and I'll take you to Harry."

He stopped and thought for a moment before adding, "Are you hungry?"

Until then, the girls had not thought about food, but they had eaten nothing since waking that morning and they were starving.

"Yes!" they shouted together. Then Eleanor remembered her manners and said, "Please may we have something to eat?"

Master John bellowed with laughter and said, "Of course you may. I'll ask Mistress Comely for something for Harry as well and now you shall have dinner for three - with something for Sophie too, I think.

"The Palace is busy tonight," he added. "Everyone is occupied and I'll have to leave you on your own with Harry, but I'm sure you'll have much to talk about. You shall come back and sleep in the kennels with me."

Master John leant down and confided, "Many would baulk at staying in the kennels with all the hounds, but it's one of the warmest and pleasantest places to be. You'll be undisturbed there until the Queen decides what to do with you. Sophie will be amongst old friends. Follow me!"

Grace and Eleanor were relieved that they had found Master John and Harry so soon, but were not too sure about the kennels and rather scared of even hearing about the Queen. The kennels were in a huge barn and it became clear that Master John lived on a gallery on the first floor, with all manner of hounds and dogs on beds on the ground floor.

It smelt very, very doggy, but as he said, it was warm and comfortable. Master John showed them to a corner of the gallery under wooden beams where they met Harry again. It seemed quite natural to them all that Sophie came upstairs with them and wasn't asked to go down with the others. She just curled up underneath the simple table.

"Now you three stay here for now. Your arrival has caused enough trouble as it is. Keep out of sight and I'll be back later," Master John told them as he banged down a tray with three steaming bowls of meaty soup and a great big bone for Sophie.

Then the three of them hugged each other before wolfing down the bowls of soup and telling each other what had happened to them.

Harry started telling his tale with a sincere apology, "I'm sorry I didn't believe what you said about The Library, Grace. It was very rude of me."

Grace was so relieved to see Harry that she had rather forgotten how mean he had been. "It's all right, Harry. It doesn't matter anymore. Tell us how you got here."

"I was woken up at about five o'clock this morning. At least I think it was this morning... coming back in time is very confusing. It was Horrible Hair Bun. She told me that Great Uncle Jasper needed to see me in his study at once and that I was to be dressed in these clothes. The trousers are very itchy."

Harry was wearing a pair of old-fashioned plus fours and a tweed jacket with a leather waistcoat. There was an old wax jacket next to him on the floor and he had some heavy leather boots on his feet.

"I was very worried. I thought something dreadful must have happened. Even Horrible Hair Bun didn't have time to be strict. She gave me a kiss goodbye." Harry touched his chin absent-mindedly and rubbed it.

"Anyway, Great Uncle Jasper was all kindness, but he said I needed to hurry…"

"'Harry,' Great Uncle Jasper had said, "I have to confide in you. What I'm about to tell you is a secret which you may share with only those who need to know. I am a member of The Witan. The Witan has been the Great Council of England for over 1,000 years and its role is to preserve the ancient freedoms of Old England. Once, before the Norman Conquest, The Witan appointed the kings of England, but since the conquest, it has stood apart and protected the peoples of England and their ancient freedoms. Often, this means working with kings and queens. Sometimes it doesn't. The Witan is a link with a much older and mystical past that few people in the modern world know about.

"'There is an old prophecy, but what I know of it is incomplete. It tells of three children who help protect the kingdom. I believe you, Grace and Eleanor are these children, but I have woken you first as the time has come for you to start your journey immediately.'"

"What do I need to do?" Harry had asked.

Then Great Uncle Jasper had carried on, "There isn't enough time to tell you everything. You must go to The Palace Library now and then leave through the Great West Door. Follow your instinct and The Library will guide you. I will try to send Eleanor and Grace after you and Edgar the Librarian will supply the books you need to help you.

"'Listen carefully, as soon as you have found the Great West Door, go through it! The Library has a way of letting

The Witan know when we need to act and the time is now. Right now. Do not let anyone delay you. Turn back through the door and find Queen Eleanor. You must trust her and you must ensure she learns to trust you equally. You'll have to be brave and quick to avoid being arrested. Tell her that you've been sent by The Witan to fulfil the Prophecy. If she doubts you, tell her you've come through The Palace Library and that the librarian's name is Edgar. Trust her. Now go!'"

At this stage in his story, Harry looked at Grace. "I'm afraid to say that I asked Great Uncle Jasper how to get to The Library then. That was when he looked at me severely and said, 'Trust Grace too. She is younger than you, but she is wise and does not tell lies. You know where to go. One last thing. You will be in a different world and time. Do not boast about your knowledge or they will think you're a magician and arrest you!'

"...I did as Uncle Jasper told me," Harry continued. "I just seemed to know where I was going and found myself in front of a huge wooden door with a smaller wooden door set into it. I opened it and found a really dark room inside. It was the Great Hall, but I didn't wait. I turned straight round and went back through the little door."

Harry took another huge mouthful of soup and chewed on the meat in it. "This is really good." His mouth was not empty as he spoke and soup dribbled down his chin.

Neither of the girls noticed, but both looked at him and said, "Don't stop. What happened next?"

"I didn't go back into The Library. It was as if the door had changed and I'd entered into a different world. I was in a field and ran straight into one of the most beautiful women

I'd ever seen, but dressed in the strangest clothes. Then I was immediately grabbed by two men who picked me up by my shoulders and held me tight. The woman looked straight at me with piercing blue eyes.

"The men were dressed in chainmail down to their knees and they seemed to be guards, but there was someone else with them. He was entirely dressed in black and he had a black triangular goatee beard.

"He leant towards me and I could smell his horrible breath, 'Who are you, boy? How dare you run into Her Majesty like that?'

"I guessed that the lady must be Queen Eleanor, so I did just what Great Uncle Jasper told me and said, 'I've been sent by The Witan to fulfil the Prophecy.'

"She looked startled at that and then she was silent for a moment. I could feel the man with the goatee beard staring at me and his mouth tightened as he said, 'Let me deal with him, Your Majesty. I can take the brat away and have him beaten for insolence.' That made me realise I was right and it was the Queen, but I certainly didn't want to be beaten.

"Then the Queen broke her silence. 'No thank you, Sir Guy. I think I can look after myself from one so young.' Then she said to one of the guards, 'Find Master John and tell him to take care of this boy and keep him in his kennels. I'll deal with him later.'

"One guard tightened his grip on me and looked at the Queen. 'Wouldn't he be safer in the dungeon?' he said.

"'No,' replied the Queen. Then she stared at me intently and leant down and whispered, 'Wait with Master John until you're called for. Speak to no one else of this. I will summon you.'

"That was only about two hours ago. I can't tell you both how happy I am to see you."

Harry gobbled the rest of his soup in double-quick time, while the girls chatted to him and tried to ask him all sorts of questions about where they were and what they were doing here. This time, he did not try to talk at the same time, but when he had finished he answered in the only way he could.

"I don't know what adventure we are on. We need to find out, but I promise to look out for you and to try not to let you down again."

Reaching across for Grace's hand, Eleanor answered him, "You're right, Harry. We're all in this together and we don't know who we can trust other than ourselves, but we all have to look out for each other, as family and friends. Let's make that our pact."

Harry reached out for Grace and Eleanor's other hands and looked at them. "I agree." At that moment, Grace felt more than ever that she had a proper family and she just nodded, too moved to speak. Then Sophie had her front paws on the table between the girls and gave a gentle whine and Grace spoke up. "Yes, Sophie. You too. We can trust you."

Master John came back to see them. He looked serious, too serious to reprimand Sophie for having her paws on the table, and said, "You must stop eating and talking now. The Queen wants you. She waits for no one and Sir Guy of Caen is downstairs waiting to escort us." More quietly, Master John added, "Sir Guy is not a man to cross or keep waiting. Come now."

7. Queen Eleanor

"The Great Sword of State has been lost forever," said Queen Eleanor to Harry, Eleanor and Grace. "It was seen being thrown overboard from the King's ship during a stormy passage from Normandy to London and His Majesty is in turmoil. It can never be recovered from the depths of the English Channel.

"Worse than that, there must be a traitor in close connection with the Court who was aboard that ship and had access to the royal treasure. The culprit wasn't seen. He hasn't been uncovered, so he may be amongst us even now."

The children had been brought to Queen Eleanor's Rooms at Clarendon Palace. Master John had told the children that the Queen was a great person in her own right. She had been Queen of France before she married the King of England and she was ruler of a land almost as large as England called Aquitaine.

"It would be as well to listen to what she has to say and obey what she commands!" said Master John, before he and

Sir Guy ushered them in to see her.

Sophie stood with the children as they had their audience with the Queen. Sir Guy was standing apart to one side. As he pushed past Sophie, the hackles on the back of her neck rose up and Eleanor noticed she gave a very low growl. It was a growl no one else could hear, but it was enough to set Eleanor wondering what was wrong.

The children could barely believe there could be more beautiful rooms in the main part of the palace. A huge fireplace with double marble columns was the centrepiece and the floor was paved with gold, grey and pink tiles.

Harry was listening carefully and thought it was time to ask a question, "Why is the Sword of State so important?"

The Queen looked at the boy for a moment as if he were a fool. Master John was quiet, but Sir Guy tut-tutted in a disapproving way.

The Queen's head turned towards him. "That will do Sir Guy." Then she sighed and explained, "The Great Sword of State was given to the kings of England before my husband's ancestor, Duke William, conquered England. It was given to them by the ruling council, The Witan, and it represents both the might and power of the King and the justice of the old and the new England. Its significance to the governance of the kingdom cannot be underestimated."

Then it was Eleanor's turn to ask a question, "Can't it just be replaced?"

This time the look of Queen Eleanor was even more withering, "Have you been taught nothing at home?" she said. Eleanor and Grace held each other's hands even more tightly.

The Queen paused and started again. "No. It cannot simply

be replaced. It is not only symbolic, but it is also magical. It has a real power which cannot be duplicated easily. In these modern times..." (at this the children looked at each other, thinking the Queen did not know the meaning of modern, but they did not dare speak) "...many people no longer believe in magic and the power of the Sword, but there are others who are well aware. There are some who say that it is King Arthur's sword, Excalibur, but it is far more likely it is St George's sword, Ascalon. The history is uncertain. No one doubts its importance.

"The loss of the Sword has made the King furious. It could not have happened at a worse time. Every person of importance in the land has been called to Clarendon to reaffirm the authority of the King and the ancient laws of England. All of them will expect to see the Sword of State and its absence could ruin everything.

"The treachery in the court must be uncovered in secret and the Sword must be replaced."

Harry now thought it was time to ask another question, even though he needed to summon up courage to do so, "I think we believe in magic. That must be what brought us here through The Palace Library, but what has this to do with us? How can we help? Surely there must be others who can do this?"

"We must replace the Sword," answered the Queen. "Or rather *you* must. The Sword can only be replaced with the help of innocents - with the help of children. That is clear in the Prophecy. The magic cannot be replicated by grown men or women."

"How can we do that?" asked Grace. "We're just children."

"You must do that with the knowledge from The Palace Library and the books that Edgar gave you. There are many secrets to making the Sword. We know a few.

"First, the Sword must be forged by an English blacksmith. We know the name of a man in Devon who is capable of doing that. Secondly, the Sword must be forged in the heat of a volcano where dragons live and breathe the hot fumes. Thirdly, the Sword must be mounted with a diamond wrestled from the oldest of the dragons. It will not be easy. There is no map to take you there, but there should be clues in your books. The King's best ship will be at your disposal. You'll need to leave tonight."

At this moment, Grace said, "Does that mean we're magicians if we can make a magic sword? Are you a magician?"

The Queen looked at her more kindly, "No we're not magicians. There are very few left in the world. I am Queen of England and Duchess of Normandy and Aquitaine. I've been Queen of France and I've visited Jerusalem on the Crusade, but I've never met a magician. It's our role to harvest the magic of the natural world.

"Be careful not to appear to be magicians. You are from a different place and time and people may believe you are witches, which would scare them and be a danger to you. People do not believe in magicians, but they believe in witches and they hate them."

The Queen then turned to Master John. "Master John, you must leave your hounds in the care of your kennelmen for some time. You will accompany these three to the King's harbour at Axmouth, where they will find the blacksmith who has been given his instructions. Then return here."

Sir Guy of Caen interrupted, which caused the Queen to frown, but he continued anyway, "Would it not be better if I, a knight, accompanied them?" Sophie's hackles rose again, but she was quiet. Only Eleanor noticed and put her hand up against the deerhound's side.

"No," said the Queen. "My decision stands. You, Sir Guy, will go ahead as quickly as possible on horseback to ensure the King's flagship is as ready as can be, although they should even now have their orders. Master John will accompany the children." She was impatient with Sir Guy and created an atmosphere in the room, which made the children think they would far rather be in Horrible Hair Bun's bad books than on the wrong side of the Queen's temper. "In fact, go now. You have the King's trust and he expects your support in this matter."

Sir Guy could do nothing except say, "Yes, Ma'am," and depart with a bow, a bow Master John thought far too short for taking leave of one's Queen.

"Do not let us down," added the Queen. "Since you enjoy the King's trust, make sure it is deserved."

As the man left the room, Eleanor felt Sophie physically relax.

"Children, I'll offer you my best wishes. You'll have to use your own initiative, but I'll wait every day to hear of your successful return.

"Harry, to you I give my signet ring. It will prove who you are and will open doors for you which would otherwise remain locked." With that she pulled a ring from her finger and slid it onto Harry's hand. It was far too big, so she turned and said, "Eloise, fetch my chain from the bedchamber so that Harry can wear this around his neck."

The children had not noticed the girl Eloise before. She had been sitting in the shadows by the fire and came forward. She would have been beautiful except a scar had disfigured her from her ear to her mouth, giving her a permanent sour smile on one side of her face. When she returned with the chain and it was slipped over Harry's neck, the Queen turned to her with sudden decision. "Eloise. You are to go with the children. I charge you with the care of their health and well-being, if necessary with your life. Be vigilant."

Eloise looked shocked and frightened, but said nothing.

To the children she turned and said, "Eloise cannot speak. She has no tongue, but she is not a dumb girl. Far from it."

"Now all of you, prepare yourselves. You must leave before midnight. Follow the valley down towards Sarum on foot and you'll find a coach waiting to take you. Above all, beware of traitors who will try to stop you."

The children were dismissed and as they left the room they felt frightened and lonely and full of questions. To make matters worse, lightning lit up the cloister and made scary shadows. Sophie kept close to them all to comfort them.

Master John tried to cheer them up, "You have the Queen's confidence and so you have my confidence too. I'm sure you will succeed and I'll look after you until we get to Axmouth, where one of the King's ships will take you to wherever you need to go."

The children knew the village of Axmouth, at least in their own time, so they hoped there would be something familiar there. And perhaps some clues.

8. The Stuffy Carriage

The children sat in a stuffy carriage after their journey on foot to Sarum. The carriage surprised them. It was quite unlike the carriages they had seen on television carrying our current Queen. This carriage was like a great big wooden box covered in metal bands and studded with great iron nails. At each corner was a wooden wheel bound with a circle of heavy steel. Each wheel was taller than Harry and the whole thing was drawn by four of the largest horses any of them had ever seen. From the outside, it looked most uncomfortable. Worse, it looked like a mobile prison.

Inside was quite another matter. Plush upholstery and rich red and blue material lined the coach. Compared to the quarters in the kennels, it was luxurious. There were no windows to look out of, but only a couple of wooden shutters to keep the cold winter weather out. In a way it was like being locked in a box, even if it was a comfortable box. Grace, Eleanor and Harry sat on one seat facing forwards. Master John and Eloise sat on the other opposite to them. Sophie was in the middle and had her head on Eleanor's lap. Master John looked quite uncomfortable sitting there, unused to the luxury of travelling in this way. Next to him sat Eloise, still looking quite terrified.

There was no time wasted getting underway and the carriage lurched and swayed along the rough roads.

It was not long before Grace asked the inevitable question that she always asked at the beginning of a journey. "How long will it take us?"

"If the road hasn't been washed away in the rain and there are no unusual delays, it should be no more than two days," answered Master John.

"Two days?" cried the children in unison. "How can it take so long?" They were quite dismayed.

"This is the finest carriage in England," said Master John, "and we're travelling under the King's protection. We won't stop except to change horses. I can never imagine the journey could be made more quickly. This carriage will be our home together until then."

To the children, it was an age. They had been thinking in modern terms and knew the journey never took more than two hours, even in traffic. They looked at each other and sighed.

"At least we can read our books to pass the time," said Eleanor.

This time it was Master John who looked surprised. "You can read?" he said. "At your age too?"

"We all can," answered Grace proudly.

"Well I admire you," he said. "I've never learnt to read books, for it is only the work of government that requires the clerics to read. I can only read my hounds and the coverts in the royal forest where we hunt. My learning is in nature and understanding what's necessary to look after the hunt."

"And can you read, Eloise?" asked Harry, trying to be polite. The girl shook her head, but made no further effort to communicate.

"We must give you your book, Harry," said Eleanor suddenly remembering. "It seems to have been such a rush that we've never had time, nor been able to tell you about our books and Edgar."

"Well, I hope they give some clues about what we have to do," replied Harry. "Let's see it," he added excitedly.

Eleanor drew the slender volume out from under her cloak and gave it to Harry. It had a plain green cover and, being patient, Harry looked at what might be written on it. There was nothing there, so he opened the first page and then the next and the next.

"What is the book?" asked the girls.

"I don't know," answered Harry. He tried not to sound irritated or disappointed. "I think it's just a notebook, there don't seem to be any words on the pages at all."

"But Edgar said it would give you wisdom when you needed it," said Grace.

"Yes," said Eleanor. "But he said something else. It was a word I didn't understand and I can't remember it. Can you Grace?"

"No."

"You're both a fat lot of good," said Harry crossly.

"I remember. I remember," answered Eleanor. "It was 'cryptic.' Do you know what that means?"

"Yes. It means it's like a puzzle. We have to work it out." He stared at the book, slightly relieved that maybe it wasn't blank after all. "Perhaps the writing is just very faint. I wish there was more light in here. Two days like this. How can we read?"

"I know," said Grace and she pulled her own book out of a pocket. She laid it on her lap and opened it up. Everyone gasped except Eleanor who knew what to expect. The inside of the carriage lit up in the same way that the dome of The Palace Library had been lit. Stars shooting out of the book were like silent fireworks. The carriage was bright with twinkling light and it was like being outside on a clear night with a full moon.

"Wow!" said Harry.

Suddenly Sophie caused mayhem. Alert almost at once from sleeping, she sat up and barked at the stars. Then she thought the best thing to do was lie on her back to look at the way the stars seemed to hover on the ceiling of the carriage. But there wasn't really room for her to manoeuvre, so as she turned she thumped her head on the door. She whined for a moment and then just comically turned her head this way and that whilst wagging her tail. She turned from noble royal dog to naughty puppy in seconds.

"Sophie!" cried Eleanor. All of a sudden the dog looked crestfallen in such a way that she changed position and sat up again, treading on all their feet in the process and placing her head on Eleanor's lap. When they finally settled down, it was Master John who spoke, "I would never have believed it, if I hadn't seen it. If I hadn't heard the Queen say that you're not magicians, I would tremble before you. But you certainly do have powerful magic. I hope you heed the Queen's advice about who you share this with."

Eloise trembled and looked worried.

"That is really cool," added Harry. Let's see if I can see any writing now. "No. Boring. You show me your book, Eleanor, anyway."

She opened up her book and showed him the beautiful pictures. As she did so, Grace tipped up her book and the stars went out, causing Sophie to bark again.

"What's happening?"

Grace put the book down flat again and they came back on, "Hey, it's like a switch," she said. "It's groovy."

"Yeah," said Harry, still annoyed that he seemed to have been given a dud book and completely uninterested in pictures of plants. Then Harry shut the book crossly and said, to no one in particular, "What are you little green book?"

Suddenly gold lettering appeared on the cover.

Peto, was the word. Then it vanished and was replaced by *Invenio*"

"It's Latin," said Harry, "but I haven't learnt these words yet. I wish they were in English."

As if responding to his wish, the gold words faded and were replaced in English: *I seek...* Then: *I find*.

"I get it I think," said Harry. "Maybe if I ask the book questions, it'll give me answers."

So Harry opened the book, as the girls looked over him. "What's my name?" he tried.

Know thyself, was the answer.

Master John was looking intently too, "Well you were told it was cryptic. Try something else."

"Where are we going?" asked Harry.

West, was the word on the page. Harry spoke it. Master John laughed out loud. "Well I could have told you that!"

"And so could I," added Grace as she pulled the gold compass and watch out of her pocket. "I must remember to wind it up each day!"

"That's beautiful," said Harry, but ignoring her really, as he was far too interested in the book now.

"Why are we going west?" tried Harry.

To fulfil the Prophecy. The three children were silent. Then Eloise seemed to recover herself and nudged Harry's knee. She looked at him and put her hands to her mouth as if she were singing.

"What do you mean?" asked Harry.

"It's no good asking Eloise that sort of question," answered Master John. "You must ask her questions she can reply 'yes' or 'no' to by nodding or shaking her head. She means read it out loud to us, since neither of us can read."

So Harry did, then he realised the next question he must ask. Great Uncle Jasper had mentioned the Prophecy and so had Queen Eleanor.

"What is the Prophecy?"

This time the book filled a whole page with words and when Harry turned the page over he found there were more. The words were in English but they were difficult to read, written in a tiny gothic script.

Speaking out loud, he strained over them. "It's a poem. I can read some of the words, but not all of them. *Dragons* is here. I wonder what that means. *Past World's End* is here. I'll have to concentrate to read this."

The journey continued as the children looked at their books in silence. For Master John and Eloise, it was late in the day and they soon fell asleep, John snoring loudly. But the three children had not only leapt in time, but missed a great chunk of the day, so they did not feel at all sleepy. Instead they turned to read each of their books.

An hour or so later, Harry declared he had deciphered the poem, but he saw that even then the girls had fallen asleep, so he closed Grace's atlas to dim the light and decided that it would have to wait until the morning.

9. The Prophecy

The movement of the great carriage could hardly be said to be rhythmic, but it was enough to lull Harry to sleep after a while. It was not as boring as being awake in the dark anyway. Strangely, it was stopping that woke them all up; or perhaps it was the shouting. There was a break to change the horses and a chance to stretch their legs. Dawn was just breaking, and since it was January and usually it was dark when the children woke up to go to school, they reckoned it must have been about seven in the morning. By the time they were back on board, they were glad of the daylight from the open shutters, even though it was bitterly cold.

Eleanor was the one who asked Harry first, "So did you manage to read the Prophecy then?"

"I did," said Harry, who was then deliberately silent for a moment.

"Well?" said Grace.

"Well what?" said Harry.

"What does it say?" asked the girls.

"Why didn't you just ask!" laughed Harry, as if it hadn't been obvious.

"Stop playing games, Harry. Just read it to us," said Eleanor crossly.

"All right, all right. Here it is. It seems to be a poem. But I must warn you, I can read the words now but I don't know what it means. It really is cryptic."

So Harry read the poem out loud to them all:

To drown the Sword not once, but twice
Will be the traitors' game.
To wreck the Crown at large
Will be the treacherous aim.

Plucked from their homes, the innocents
Will travel past World's End
To meet their destiny and fate
To rescue freedom and a friend.

Hell's Bay will sound with clashing tones.
Dragons must not be slain
When fire heats up the water's edge
When Ascalon is forged again.

By Dragons' Bane the children three
Will dull and lull the putrid lair,
To pluck from him the oily stone
By breathing out the vapoured air.

Box up your fears and frights,
Beware the direct route.
Success will come to he who thinks,
Who wears another's suit.

The traitors' curse will free itself
When passions clash with fate.
Freedom and not the end
Lies through the Traitors' Gate.

The Witan looks for freedom first.
Seek and you will find.
Trust in the truth; look for knowledge.
May friendship be your bind.

"Is that it?" said Grace. "I don't understand. What's it meant to mean?"

"Well," added Master John. "It's certainly a pretty piece. Parts seem clear, but most of it is very cloudy. Now at least we know that if Queen Eleanor knew part of the Prophecy, she knew enough that there was a drowned sword and three children.

"It seems clear too that you're on a hunt as well - a dragon hunt - as the Queen warned you. Perhaps there are clues in this, perhaps not. We have another day in this carriage so there'll be plenty of time for you to think about it anyway."

Eloise, of course, sat silently throughout this. But Sophie was sitting up in the carriage, her nose up high sniffing the air and listening intently, before she put her head down on Eleanor's lap. Eleanor fondled Sophie's head absent-mindedly.

61

"Read the verse with the bit about the dragon again will you, Harry?"

"Hell's Bay will sound…"

"No not that one. The next one."

"By Dragons' Bane, the children three
Will dull and lull the putrid lair,
To pluck from him the oily stone…"

"Dragons' Bane. I thought so," said Eleanor. "I've seen the word 'bane' before in my book. I just need to find it again."

Eleanor flicked through the book and found the right page. "Here it is." She began reading, "*Purple Bane. A beautiful and delicate flower once believed to have been common all over England, but now very rare. It has delicate flowers which tempt you to smell it, but the plant stinks. What bane it was used for is now forgotten, but it serves no modern purpose.*' I think 'bane' means poison. Perhaps Dragons' Bane is how we kill the dragons to get the diamond."

"But the poem says that dragons must not be slain," pointed out Harry. "Perhaps the dragons need to be alive for the magic to work on the Sword. Maybe the blacksmith will know when we meet him."

"Not all poisons kill," replied Master John. "The healers sometimes mix up herbs and flowers for my hounds if they need looking after. It makes them drowsy and can put them to sleep. They are poisons sure enough, but do not kill. When they awake, they seem to recover. You need to talk to a healer and ask more about this Dragons' Bane. Perhaps one could tell you."

"More to the point," said Grace, "it doesn't seem to tell us where we're going. I'm learning to use my star map to help us get somewhere, but it's not much good if we don't even know where we're going! World's End sounds a little scary, but not as bad as Hells' Bay. I don't think I want to go to either!"

Master John leant forward and put a hand on her knee. "You may not want it, but meeting your 'destiny and fate' won't often coincide with anything you want to do. Look at how you ended up here."

The children looked at each other. However kindly the words were meant, none of them found them very comforting. At the same time, Sophie sat up with one paw on Harry and Eleanor's legs. She licked – well, kissed really - Grace's hand before settling down across all of their toes. That, at least, was comforting.

"I'm sure I've heard of Hell's Bay before," said Grace. "I've just got to remember where."

"Well do let us know when you remember," answered Harry, a little irritably.

Grace stuck her tongue out at him, which at least made her feel a little better. And Eloise smiled at that, wishing she had a tongue to stick out at all.

10. Eleanor's Book

"What is that disgusting smell?" shouted Grace.

They had all been snoozing. It was the afternoon of the second day and they had suffered a bad night in the carriage, uncomfortable and unable to sleep. Late that morning, they had turned off the road onto a much better road at a place called Ilchester.

By then, Grace felt she was beginning to master her star charts. Harry knew the Prophecy off by heart now and kept asking his book questions, but also kept getting a bit fed up with just how cryptic the answers were. In the back of his mind, he was a bit cross about it all, as he couldn't work it out.

Eleanor knew about hundreds of plants and what the book said they were used for. There were plants for healing cuts, plants to stop you feeling hungry, and plants for curing animals. But she was fed up too. Her book didn't seem to be at all magical like the others.

The few times they had changed horses, there had been

little more than five minutes to stretch their legs and to accept whatever parcels of food were given to them. Sometimes it was delicious; sometimes it seemed rank. Mead had been offered, and Master John had made them drink it in places he knew the water to be foul. It was sweet like honey, but a little bitter too. And it was alcoholic. All three children had the strange sensation of being tipsy for the first time. It was enough to quench their thirst before the watchful Eloise snatched the heady potion away from them. Then, they had dozed off. Perhaps it was the mead.

Grace had woken them all with her shout. "It's a really, really horrid smell," she added.

"Yuck," said Harry and Eleanor at once. Then Harry added for good measure, "That's a really disgusting fart." They giggled.

Even Eloise smiled at that, though she pretended not to and held her nose shut with her fingers.

Master John then stood up, as far as the short ceilings in the carriage would allow, and threw open the shutters: "January it may be and the air may be freezing cold, but we need some fresh air."

Just then, a huge pothole threw him down on the lap of Eloise. She squealed, but he just bellowed with laughter. "I'm cooped up in here with you all. Now the fresh air is giving me strength. God help me if they don't give me a horse on my own in the open to ride back to Clarendon!"

The smell was not much better, and Sophie barked, just once. Eloise pointed at Eleanor and she looked down. The sun streaming into the carriage from the open shutters had blinded them all for a moment, but they saw what it was now.

Sophie's paws were on Eleanor's book and she seemed to be scratching the page with them.

"Is it you making that smell, Sophie?" asked Harry. Her response to that was to put her ears back and give a little friendly growl which clearly meant: "No it's not. Don't be rude."

Then Eleanor jabbed Harry and pointed at the book, "Look, silly."

Sophie scratched the book again. The picture seemed to lift off the page. It was as if the plant was actually growing out of the book and wafting gently in the wind. It had beautiful purple flowers. But it seemed to be smoking. It filled the carriage with a misty vapour. It stank.

"It's the Purple Bane," said Eleanor. "The one they say really smells."

"I know what to do with that then," said Grace. She leant over and pushed Sophie off the book, before turning the page. All of a sudden, the misty vapour was sucked back into the book and the smell vanished. Everything just went back into the book.

"That's better," said Master John. Eloise took her fingers off her nose and sniffed the air.

"See," said Grace smugly.

"I do have a magic book!" said Eleanor, suddenly happy and not feeling left out at all. "It's a scratch and sniff book!" She flicked over the pages, found what she was looking for and frantically began scratching the page. Up sprang a beautiful rose bush with the prettiest pink flowers. Then the carriage filled with the most beautiful smell of summer roses, but no smoky mist this time. They all felt a lot better.

Eleanor scratched vigorously. "Ouch," she suddenly said. "There's a thorn in my finger." Everyone just laughed unfairly, as Eleanor put her finger in her mouth to stop the prick of blood. The only one who seemed to give her any attention was Eloise. Quickly she found something from under the folds of her robe and leant forward. She gently pulled Eleanor's finger from her mouth and bandaged the wound. It was only a little prick, but Eleanor smiled and thanked her. To Eleanor, this shy girl suddenly seemed to have a personality beyond her timid presence in the carriage.

"Where are we now?" asked Grace. "Is it far to go?"

"Not far," replied Master John. "We turned onto the Fosse Way at Ilchester and soon we will soon be at Axmouth, the end of that great road. It is one of the busiest ports on the south coast."

"What's the Fosse Way?" asked Grace.

"The Fosse Way, young Grace, is one of the greatest roads in the kingdom. It runs in a straight line from Lincoln to Axmouth and was built by the Romans. It's not like our happy little winding English lanes and ways. It's a great road that has carried armies and commerce across the kingdom for centuries. I doubt there will be a better road built in our lifetime."

At that the children smiled to themselves, but heeding the advice of the Queen, they kept quiet, even in front of Master John and the nervous Eloise.

Master John carried on: "At Axmouth there's a great estuary and port and the King's finest ship awaits your instructions. I hope you're prepared now after consulting your magical books."

Master John had been listening to their conversations,

and he thought they had been making progress. But within themselves, the children were full of doubt. None of them was entirely sure they were any the wiser about the task they had been set. Harry didn't think that he had used his book wisely enough and Grace suddenly had a guilty feeling that all the time she had been reading her own book she should have been trying to remember where Hell's Bay was. She was sure she knew.

"When we arrive, we must travel up the valley to find the blacksmith. He's been warned. Then I must return in the morning."

"The blacksmith?" asked Eleanor.

"Aye. You remember. The Queen told you a message had been sent ahead to meet the Englishman who will help forge the new sword."

"Do you have to leave us?" said Harry quietly, echoing the thoughts of the others, including Eloise. His boisterous humour had kept them in good spirits during the journey, even though his huge size meant that sometimes he dominated their small space.

"I do. My place is with the Royal Hunt and with His Majesty the King. I must return as soon as I've delivered you to Axmouth. I'll take you to the blacksmith and then I must leave you."

"After that," he bellowed with laughter, "the Captain of the King's flagship will have to take orders from you, Grace. For you have a skill of navigation which will leave him overwhelmed, in spite of all his experience!"

11. The Blacksmith

"Do you think he is a real dwarf?" whispered Grace to Eleanor.

"Yes," the short man shouted at them as they quivered under the thatched overhang at the forge. Rain was now dripping off them since a sudden storm and squall had soaked them all as they walked through the village. "He's a real dwarf with very, very sharp hearing."

They looked at him - not up at him, which made a change for children of their age when speaking to an adult - and the smiles on their faces turned to fear. Then Eleanor realised that they were probably just being rude by whispering, so she said "We're sorry for whispering. Mummy says we shouldn't. I'm Eleanor. This is my brother Harry and our cousin Grace."

"Well how do you do then, Eleanor and Grace." He still looked very bad-tempered. He was not much taller than Harry, but about three times as wide, with a chaotic red beard and a mad mop of red hair. A heavy leather apron was wrapped round him from his neck to his feet. Great chunks of his beard seemed to be singed and missing, the effect of burns.

"Well you are very small to be the solution to this kingdom's problems." Then he let out a hollow laugh and the girls were not quite sure to make of it. They were not sure if it was a joke or if he was being serious.

Master John stepped in under the thatch, nearly bending double, and thrust his hand out to shake the dwarf's. "I am Master John of the Royal Hunt. I assume you are Master Edwin of Axmouth, the blacksmith and armourer?"

"I am," was the reply. "But how should I know you are who you say you are," he added.

"You have heard of the Prophecy?" asked Master John.

"I have."

"Then these are the three children."

"Well they don't look up to much," carried on the blacksmith. "Three healthy children for sure, but how do we know they are not impostors?"

This was almost too much for Master John, and bending nearly double he looked the dwarf in the eye. He used a tone the children had not heard before, "I know, as our Queen put them into my charge."

The dwarf looked him straight back in the eye and said, "But I was not there."

At that moment, Harry realised he had the solution to this problem, and he pulled at the chain around his neck.

"Here is the Queen's signet ring, Sir. It is her token and our authority to be here."

Edwin looked at the signet ring and looked almost disappointed that they were not traitors for him to dispose of as he wished. "Well you seem to be what you say you are. You'd better come in."

The inside of the forge was much bigger than the overhanging eaves they had crowded under outside. It was a huge room, with a furnace at one end, surrounded by all the blacksmith's tools. There were great iron hammers and tongs hanging on beams above. At the other end, nearest the door, was a more traditional hearth and fireplace, with a pot hanging over the fire and some sort of soup bubbling away in it. A half-open door at the back led to a cramped room to sleep in.

"Welcome to my home. This is my wife, Anwen." The words were a little grudging, but at least they were welcomed inside. As if to put a stop to his initial impression of grumpiness, the dwarf said, "We are proud of our home and workshop. It is the only stone house in the village, the only stone building until the church was put up some years ago. And it's warm enough with the furnace and the fire both going. Anwen will look after you."

At that, Edwin drew up a chair away from the kitchen hearth and started rocking it back and forth, watching what was going on.

Anwen gently welcomed them and took their wet cloaks from them. "He'll have your interests at heart now he knows who you are, but he will be grumpy."

"Humph!" came a grunt from the chair.

Anwen looked small standing next to Master John, but huge when she was next to her husband. She smiled, revealing several missing teeth, but just added, "Who's hungry?"

"Me," shouted Harry, adding 'please' for good measure. And the girls realised they were too.

Just then, before they had time to react, Edwin leapt up

from his chair. He pulled the dagger from Eleanor's scabbard where it hung round her waist. It had been revealed after her long cloak had been taken off. He held it up to the light and then towards her, shaking angrily. "Where did you get this dagger? I'd know it anywhere. I made it for Queen Eleanor herself only three years ago." He looked at the blade carefully and almost spoke to himself. "It is worn more than it should have been, but it is the one."

Then turning to his wife, Edwin added, "Look at the blade, Anwen. It glows green, as well it might in the presence of danger or traitors. It is definitely the one." Turning to Eleanor again, he said, "Where did you get this blade?"

Now Eleanor may have been frightened, but she did have enough presence of mind not to give away anything about The Palace Library to a stranger. Just at that moment, she wondered whether Edwin might be a traitor himself. She was just working out what to say, when Master John stepped before him and gently said, "You've seen the Queen's signet ring. This is clearly a gift from the Queen as well. It's not our place to question her, or these children from the Prophecy."

"Master John is right, husband," added Anwen. "Be calm and accept we are in the companionship of those we expected to see for this journey. Your task is a burdensome one, to reforge the Great Sword of State and renew Ascalon. Be helpful to these three who have far less experience, but must help you."

The dwarf looked round and then relaxed. "You're right as ever, Anwen." He turned the dagger and returned it to Eleanor. "Bring me one of your comforting infusions of herbs and rid me of this temper of mine. Then we'll plan our journey together over supper."

Anwen ground up some dried herbs from the side with a pestle and infused them in boiling water before passing Edwin a plain earthenware cup. He drank deeply from it and seemed to physically relax back into his chair. Then he sat up again, and in a completely different tone he turned to Eleanor, "I am sorry," he said.

Eleanor had been watching this all intently - the mixing of the herbs and the effect it had on Edwin. "That's OK," she said sweetly. The she turned to Anwen and said, "Are you a healer then?"

"Some people say so, but I am no magician. I just understand plants and how to use them."

"I have a book of plants. Can I show it to you?"

"A book?" replied Anwen. "That's a rare thing and I wouldn't know how to read it."

"It has pictures!" said Eleanor.

Master John interrupted with admiration, "All these children are rare things. They all have books. They can all read words, and doubtless write them too. If your magic is plants, Master Edwin's is with the forge and mine is with hounds, then each of these children has a gift within themselves and their books."

"Well, we'll see it soon enough," said Edwin, quite cheerfully now, and taking charge within his own house. "First let's eat. Then we'll have a council and make our plans. Then you can read your books. The King's ship awaits us all and will leave on the high tide tomorrow afternoon. We have until then to plan."

So they ate a delicious stew - wild boar - and even though the forge was really a tiny building, they all marvelled at the space they had after living in the cramped carriage for two days. Then Anwen gave them a hot drink and said, "This will keep us alert while we talk tonight, and then afterwards we will all sleep well. It may be your last night on dry land for some time."

Harry then asked, "Where are we going? It seems we must go by sea, but do you know where we're going?"

"Humph!" muttered Edwin, settling back into his grumpy ways, before being sharply pulled up by a look from Anwen.

"I hoped you could tell us that," Edwin added. "First however, I'll remind you why we're going. I have to forge a new Sword of State since traitors near the King's person have destroyed the other. This must not be forged here in my workshop, but in the heat of the volcano, where dragons live. The heat is needed to pass on the power of Ascalon."

"Who is Ascalon?" asked Grace, simply. She thought it was time someone asked as they had heard the name several times and it was in the Prophecy. It was time they all stopped pretending they knew.

"It is not who, young Grace, but what!" replied Edwin. "Ascalon was the lance that St George used in his famous battle with the dragon."

"You'd better tell us the story then Edwin," said Anwen. So Edwin took another sip at his drink and told the story.

"There are many versions of the tale told, but few will know the truth as well as I do." The children looked at Edwin with interest. Sitting at the table, his height made no difference, and his presence was powerful.

"Many centuries ago, George was a powerful merchant and warrior. Dragons were even then rare in England. He lived in a part of the kingdom where there was one powerful dragon that had a hold over the villages and towns all around. They were forced to sacrifice sheep to the dragon and when the sheep no longer satisfied the dragon's hunger, for there were not enough, they drew lots to sacrifice their daughters.

"George was passing through and had fallen in love with one of daughters in the village - the daughter of the Lord of the Manor - and swore that he would save the villagers. He told them they must not sacrifice any more sheep or children to the dragon, for it was not God's wish. He would challenge the dragon. They locked up the towns and the villages to keep everyone safe and George went out in search of the dragon with his armour and his finery.

"What most stories will tell you is that he then destroyed the dragon but in fact he could not. He fought and fought, but he was losing, so he withdrew. He was full of doubt and fear. So he went down to the river and prayed."

"Did that help?" asked Grace a little doubtfully.

"Of course!" smiled Edwin. "For he found a dwarf who was a blacksmith! Hah! Now everyone knows dwarves are the best blacksmiths and armourers, but that does not mean everyone likes us. This blacksmith lived by the river, as even then people were frightened of dwarves and we were not welcome to live within the villages or towns, which you will remember were all locked up.

"That dwarf was called Edwin," said Edwin with some pride.

"Was that you?" asked Grace simply, since she alone with the other two children was now used to the idea of Edgar the Librarian being nearly 1,000 years old.

75

"No, of course not," said Edwin, brushing off the comment. "I said it was centuries ago. But he was my direct ancestor."

"George regained some of his confidence from resting and praying by the river, but he realised he needed to put away his fears and his doubts. The dwarf offered him new armour, but George said any armour would be too heavy and too hot when the dragon threw out flames from his mouth.

"Instead, George asked the dwarf to melt down his armour and make a box out of it. The dwarf was a bit surprised at this, but he was persuaded and so the box was made. George then said he would put all his fears into the box, along with all his doubts and his lack of faith. Then he would face the dragon again and conquer him.

"Now the dwarf tried to persuade him otherwise, but George would not listen. In the end though, the dwarf persuaded him to carry a lance - a lance that had been forged for a great king in the past at the foot of a volcano and with all the magic that imparts. That lance was called Ascalon."

"Then George went out and conquered the dragon. Thereafter he married the Lord of the Manor's daughter and led a simple life of faith with her.

"The dragon wasn't conquered simply by the lance, but by George's faith and confidence. The dragon wasn't killed. In spite of all the evil it had committed, it was given mercy - in return for all dragons being banished from England forever. So now there are no dragons in England at all. Instead they were sent to the edge of Hell, never to be seen by man again. They were imprisoned forever by the faith of St George and also by their greed, as they took their stolen treasure with them, since, as everyone knows, dragons are great hoarders. Keeping that, it seemed worthwhile to forego eating the sheep and the daughters of England, even though such abstinence makes the dragons hungry and angry.

"While England is protected by the Sword of State and the power of Ascalon and the faith of St George, its freedoms are protected and the dragons cannot return."

"So", said Harry, beginning to understand some of the Prophecy a little more, but wishing he didn't. "We have to travel by sea as the dragons aren't in England. And we must go to the edge of Hell. To Hell's Bay."

"Yes," said Edwin simply. Then he added sarcastically, "That is all."

Then they all stayed silent, nervous and apprehensive, except Grace, who suddenly remembered where Hell's Bay was.

12. The Healer

"What on earth are you doing? You'll burn yourself," said Master John, standing up and bumping his head on a low wooden beam across the ceiling.

Master Edwin, the blacksmith and armourer, had sat back in his chair while they all digested his story and Harry's comments about going to the edge of Hell.

"Relax, Master John. I'm used to the heat of the furnace. As Anwen well knows. She treats enough of my burns. The fire relaxes me and it helps me think."

Edwin pulled a small wooden bowl off the shelf. It was attached to a narrow tube, and he filled the bowl with herbs from a jar. It was when he pulled a burning ember from the fire and set fire to the herbs that John stood up and questioned him.

"It's just a pipe," said Harry. "I've seen Great Uncle Jasper with one before."

The room filled with a cloudy smoke. It was a sweet smell

with the herbs burning. It disguised the smell of the forge and the food they had eaten for dinner.

"Relax, Master John," said Anwen. "It helps him think."

The dwarf continued puffing on his pipe, pleased with his story. Eleanor had been learning about the discovery of America at school before and she whispered to Grace, "I don't think they've invented tobacco yet. It's not surprising John is alarmed!"

But Grace was not listening.

"I remember where Hell's Bay is," she said. "We went there last summer for our holidays. It was when I first really got to know you both."

They were all wide awake now. Whether it was the excitement or Anwen's potion, they didn't know; they didn't care.

"You mean in Scotland?" asked Harry, remembering the fun time they had all had there with his and Eleanor's parents and friends.

"No, no, before that. Don't you remember? Before that."

Harry and Eleanor looked at Grace as if she were simple, a younger cousin who didn't know much, but she had the better memory this time.

"Come on, we sat at the beach looking at the island opposite with the sun going down every night."

They still looked blank.

"You were sick on the boat, Eleanor. You must remember that!"

"I certainly do," she replied. "That was the wrong way to travel!"

"That doesn't bode well," commented Edwin, puffing on

the pipe again, but they ignored him.

"The island opposite had a place called Hell's Bay. That's where I've heard of it before."

This time, Edwin sat up. "You really mean you've been there before?"

Grace looked around, uncertain how to answer. 'Before' was certainly not accurate, given they had jumped back in time, but she was nervous about sharing this, especially after what the Queen had said. So Grace answered a different question, thinking about the time she had spent on the boat overnight (not being sick) and looking at the stars.

"We went west from here. The sun always set in the west. Then we went across the sea and went to some islands. They were beautiful. That was where Hell's Bay was."

"Beauty and the edge of Hell. That doesn't exactly match. Are you sure?" said Edwin.

"Yes, yes. I know."

"Humph!"

Harry was the next to speak. "It does make sense. We went past Land's End. That's where we saw the dolphins. What if Land's End is the same as World's End in the Prophecy? As far as England is concerned, the end of Cornwall is the end of the world. I bet Grace has put us on the right path. We can get there by boat. They aren't so far away to persuade the Captain to go there."

"But I don't remember a volcano there," said Eleanor.

"No," said Grace, "but remember it's nearly a thousand years ahead."

The children looked around, worrying their secret had been let out. Anwen and Eloise looked at them suspiciously, but said nothing. Master John simply sat quietly. Master Edwin puffed at his pipe, as if he had noticed nothing.

Then he said, "Well, that at least is a plan. We head west tomorrow." They nodded in agreement, not least since no one had any better idea. "That's the first thing this council has concluded.

"Now you had better see St George's box." It seemed he had really decided to trust them. Perhaps the pipe had done him some good.

Edwin stood up and went around the back of his furnace, before bringing out a rectangular metal box. It didn't look like much: just a plain metal box.

"Is that really the box?" asked Eleanor, suddenly enchanted.

"It is," replied Edwin. "It's not so much the box that matters, but what it contains. After George subdued the dragon and had him in his power, the lance, Ascalon, broke into pieces. Many, many tiny pieces. Its job was done, but the power it had was retained in all the smaller pieces. My ancestor Edwin spent weeks collecting them from the ground. They were difficult to find as the blade splintered. Within this box, are the pieces that are left. They've been handed down from father to son for generations and are in my care. My great great grandfather placed one in the blade of the Sword of State that is now lost. That was annealed in a volcano, but I don't know how. I was privileged to place a piece in the dagger you wear, Eleanor, but that was never annealed in the volcano. It hasn't the same power."

Edwin opened the box. The pieces within glowed green, just as Eleanor's dagger had before. He looked up at Anwen. "I've never seen them this bright before. There is much danger and treachery about, but that's no surprise in the circumstances. We must all watch out. For ourselves and each other. And we must have eyes in the back of our heads." He looked harsh.

They all looked around the table, suddenly uncertain of who to trust. The children knew and loved each other well, but what did they know of all these others? Eloise was difficult to get to know since she could not speak, but Edwin had proven to be grumpy and difficult. Did he trust them? Should they trust him? Master John was a cheerful soul and Edgar had told them about him, but was he leading them astray? It was hard to know.

It was Sophie who broke the atmosphere. She pushed her nose up at Eleanor's pocket to reveal her book of plants. Eleanor looked at her and realised what she was saying. It was time for her to talk to Anwen about plants, herbs and healing. It was not the first time Eleanor thought that Sophie had a clearer judgement about who to trust and who not to. Perhaps it was the sense of empathy that Edgar had spoken about. Eleanor remembered she must speak to Harry and Grace about the way Sophie had behaved when Guy of Caen had pushed past them in their audience with the Queen. She would need a moment alone.

Eleanor stood up and moved to sit with Anwen and show her the book. "It's time for me to show you my book. I think it's important and it's special too. I have read it, but you have the experience. Will you help me?"

"Of course I will," said Anwen. "You have a difficult journey ahead of you and you will have to learn to be the healer."

"Aren't you coming with us?" asked Eleanor.

"No. I cannot. But come over here and let's see what I can

pack for you and teach you."

Eleanor still wasn't quite sure whether to show her all the secrets of the book after the discussion about treachery, but Sophie decided things for her. She flicked the book out of her hands on to the floor and started scratching at the page it opened. A lavender bush seemed to grow out of the book and the room became full of a soothing fragrance.

"Clever dog," said Anwen, unsurprised at the magic of the book. "That will soothe all our nerves."

"She's called Sophie," said Eleanor. "A man called Edgar sent her with us, but I think she belongs to the Queen too."

"Perhaps," said Anwen, "she is wiser than us all at the moment. Come. We will pack some herbs and plants."

Anwen seemed to move all around the room gathering dried herbs and plants from everywhere. Eleanor followed and listened. "This is good for sea sickness. It sounds like you will need that," Anwen said. Then, she looked affectionately at Edwin and said, "These are good for burns if you mix then with mead. I know all about them from treating Edwin after his work at the furnace!" They spent several hours at this.

Whilst Eleanor and Anwen looked through their book and prepared potions in the kitchen, Grace had fallen asleep and Master John had carried her to a straw mattress at the back.

Harry read his book, quietly asking it questions. But whenever he said, "Where are we going?" the pages just said *Peto* and *Invenio* as if they'd forgotten how to speak English. He was fed up with it again.

The storm outside had settled down and it was not long before they were all asleep on straw mattresses on the floor.

13. Dragons' Bane

In the late morning, Eleanor walked ahead with Anwen, clutching a bag of dried herbs and spices, which they had supplemented with fresh pickings from the hedgerows.

Grace and Harry walked behind talking to each other. Master John had stayed behind with Master Edwin to pack his heavy tools into a cart and bring them down to the Harbour Inn, where he had promised to meet them to make their farewells.

The forge was outside the main part of the village and the night before they had barely seen Axmouth at all.

"Edwin is rather scary isn't he?" Grace said to Harry. "Do you think he is the traitor?"

"Well, I wouldn't think so," replied Harry. "He calmed down a lot after first meeting us and seemed to be helpful. But I suppose he could have been just pretending. Anyway the Queen seems to trust him, even if no one else does."

"But that's the whole point, isn't it?" replied Grace. "You trust people and then they turn out to be a traitor and let you down."

"I suppose so," said Harry. "But how could he be the traitor? He can't have been on the ship when the Sword was thrown overboard. But on the other hand the Prophecy talks about traitors, not one but more. Maybe there's a conspiracy. What do you think of Eloise? She's seems to be a dark one."

"But she's the Queen's private maid. And I think she's sweet," said Grace.

"Sweet?" said Harry. "With that funny face and the sort of moody silence."

"Well you can't exactly blame her for being silent with a missing tongue or for that scar. Anyway, she was giggling when you talked about a fart in the carriage. Most adults don't do that. Sophie has a feeling for people too and she hasn't growled at her."

"But Sophie hasn't exactly been affectionate to her either. Who could it be then?" asked Harry. "Master John?" They both agreed it was unlikely to be him. Anyway, they liked him too much. "He just seems too honest and easy to read," added Harry.

"It's that Guy of Caen that I didn't like," said Grace, "but we've seen so little of him, it's not exactly fair to judge."

"We had better just be very careful and keep an eye out for ourselves. At least we know each other," added Harry as they turned the corner towards the River Axe.

The village didn't look like the Axmouth the children knew, but they could hardly expect it to. But they saw the lie of the land and recognised the big hills around them, with the old - or not so old - hill fort up above them. What surprised them all was how busy the little place was, with all sorts of inns and activity. It was a major port, Master John had said. But neither of them could imagine how the river they knew with its mud flats at low tide could possibly be a major port, even with a thousand years of difference. A few people looked at them strangely, especially at Harry's plus fours and wax jacket, but when they saw they were with Anwen, the dwarf's wife, they soon turned away. These were different people, and there were often strangers in the place too.

Then the children saw the ship moored up beyond the Harbour Inn. It was quite unlike anything they had seen before and looked magnificent. There were two masts, one at the front and one towards the back. Gold and red lantern sails hung from them both. Then at the back of the ship - the stern - was a high poop deck with castellations around the side and living quarters below. Each side had holes for huge oars.

But soon, they noticed the river and it distracted them from the boat.

Eleanor ran to them, "Look at the river. It must be half a mile wide and Anwen says it's really deep. That's why this is such an important place. The ships can come up here and park away from the bay when it's stormy. It's amazing."

Anwen looked slightly bemused. She had lived in the village all her life and took it for granted. "It's the way it has been and always will be," she said.

"Edwin will be some time. Come and look at the church. That was only built a few years ago."

Inwardly the children sighed. That was no fun and there was so much else to see, with the harbour to explore and the ship to look at. They had spent so much time cooped up too; they just wanted to run around.

"There's a mural of St George on the wall too," said Anwen, trying to encourage them some more. "See if you can spot what's different from Edwin's story. I don't think the painter can have heard his tale when he drew it, but that much can't be helped. Edwin's always grumpy when he sees it!"

So they followed her into the church. It was tiny and dark, with stained glass windows in dark blue and red. It took a while for their eyes to become accustomed to the light before they could see the mural on the wall. The children stared at it.

"St George shouldn't be wearing armour," said Harry. "It was too hot and too heavy for him to wear with all the dragon's flames. But I can see the lance, Ascalon!"

Grace added, "And the dragon is dead. It should have surrendered to St. George."

"You are both right," laughed Anwen. "You see, the church is not so boring!"

It was Eleanor who had the sharpest eyes though. She pointed to a purple flower at the base of the picture. "That's the Purple Bane, the smelly flower from my book!"

"I've never seen it in real life," said Anwen, "and few people believe it actually exists, even amongst healers. It's in all the pictures of St George I've ever seen. I know it by another name: Dragons' Bane."

"Dragons' Bane," gasped the children. Then Harry added, "That's in the Prophecy." He knew it all by heart now and quoted the verse:

"By Dragons' Bane, the children three
Will dull and lull the putrid lair,
To pluck from him the oily stone
By breathing out the vapoured air."

"Yes," carried on Anwen. "The myth I've heard says it only grows where dragons live, so it's no surprise that I've never seen it. A bane is a poison, but I suppose where there is an evil like a dragon, nature may provide a protection nearby. It's like finding a dock leaf in the same place that a nettle has stung you. One provides relief for the other."

Eleanor was thinking and had pulled the book from the inner pocket of her cloak, flicking through the pages to find the picture of the Purple Bane.

"Oh please don't," said Grace. "It smells like a fart." Harry giggled.

A priest was heading towards them. "It's time to go outside," said Anwen quickly.

"The priest doesn't like what I do with plants and herbs," whispered Anwen. "He says faith should be enough to heal, but I believe nature is part of God's world. In any case, as a woman, I shouldn't be in the church alone with you or anyone. Let's go."

She closed the book for Eleanor, and they headed back into the daylight, blinking as they went.

"Eleanor," said Anwen as they walked, "you must learn what this Dragons' Bane does when you arrive at Hell's Bay. With some plants, it is enough to touch them to implant their power. With others you must dry them and crush them. Others must be immersed in water. Others must be burnt to inhale the fumes. Use your book and what I've taught you."

As they left the grounds of the church, Anwen seemed to relax.

"Stop!" shouted Grace.

"What is it?" asked Harry.

"We never visit this church without visiting Grandpa's grave. We should go back."

"But he hasn't even been born yet," whispered Harry. "It's 1164. There is no grave."

"But there will be," said Eleanor.

"You're right," answered Harry after thinking for a moment. "Will be or was or is. It doesn't matter. Let's go." They turned, but after a moment, Harry looked at Anwen and said. "We won't be long. Can you wait?"

"Of course. I'll wait in the inn."

The three children went around to the south side of the church where their grandfather would be buried and found a patch of rough wintery grass. "It's here I think," said Grace.

"Shall we say a prayer?" asked Harry.

"I don't know what to say," said Grace.

"Nor do I," answered, Harry. "Let's just stay silent for a moment, shall we?"

They all knelt down and Sophie sat beside them too, with her head bowed.

After a minute, Eleanor said. "I wish we had some flowers. I'm going to try something." She took the book out again and turned to the lavender. Then she flicked across the page, just as Edgar the Librarian had when he gave them their purple cloaks.

They all looked. Suddenly it seemed as if a flurry of air lifted something off the page and settled on the ground. They stared for a minute longer, but nothing happened.

"It was worth a try, Eleanor," said Harry. "I think Grandpa would have liked that."

They moved quietly away from the church, a little

disappointed by the lack of magic. What they would never know is that a beautiful lavender plant emerged there the following June. The priest would never know how it came to be there, but he tended it anyway.

14. The Saint George

The smell assaulted the noses of the three children when they first boarded the boat. They were glad of their little leaving gift from Anwen; three little cloth bags full of scented herbs. Now they knew what they were for. Even Harry, who thought it was a bit girly, held the bag to his nose to disguise the horrid smells. There was the smell of raw sewage, which hung over the air alongside the smell of sweaty bodies. Then there was the rotting offal from the abattoir that stood by the quayside to supply the ships with meat. They weren't even sure that the smell of Purple Bane or Dragons' Bane scratched from Eleanor's book might not be better. Poor Sophie with her sensitive nose didn't have a cloth bag, but Eleanor sat down with her from time to time and shared her own. The deerhound breathed in the scent of the cloth bag deeply through her nose before lying down again and panting through her mouth to avoid the nauseous smells going up her nostrils.

The children were standing right up on the poop deck at

the back of the boat - or the stern, as they soon learned to call it. There had been tears from the girls when they said goodbye to Master John and Anwen on the quayside. Even Harry had been very silent and upright when he shook Master John's hand, feeling little wells of water forming in the corner of his eyes.

Edwin was down on the main deck, organising his tools and belongings to his own satisfaction. Eloise was below the decks, making up the Captain's cabin, which had been handed over to Eleanor, Grace and Eloise for the journey. Harry was to sleep in a hammock in a tiny cabin with Edwin, while the Captain would make do with a cot in his chart room. But these were all places of supreme comfort compared to rest of the crew, who simply had to find a space to hang a hammock anywhere they could, sometimes on the open deck.

If Harry had been asked to describe how the Captain of the King's flagship might have looked, he might have imagined a man in a long blue coat with gold braid and smart white trousers. But the man who had welcomed them aboard looked more like a pirate than the captain of his imagination. A hook and a parrot on the shoulder would not have seemed strange.

"I don't like the look of the Captain," said Eleanor. "His eyes never seem to stay still. They look around the place all the time."

"I don't know how we can tell," said Harry. "He seems to be doing so much all at once getting ready to leave." Harry had had the sense to show the Captain the Queen's signet ring at once when they arrived. They had been expected and there was little trouble getting on board.

"Once we are underway down the river with the oars, you

can tell me our destination and we will plot a course. We must leave within an hour with the ebb of the high tide." These were just about the only words the Captain had uttered to them when they arrived.

"I tell you who I really don't like," confided Eleanor. "It's Guy of Caen. He came aboard just as we were leaving. He looked all self-important and well-dressed in the wrong sort of way with all that dark black. He had nasty tight lips. The Captain didn't seem that pleased to see him either. And he smells funny."

"What do you mean smells funny? It's not as if anyone around here exactly smells nice. I don't think anyone washes in 1164," said Harry. "Give us a few more days and we won't be smelling that nice. Mind you, he did have terrible breath when I first came across him."

"I can't pin it down, but Master John smelt all doggy and a bit ripe, but it was comforting. Guy of Caen smells off. Most of all though, Sophie doesn't like him."

"How do you know that?"

"I've been meaning to tell you ever since we left the carriage, but this is the first time we've been alone together. When we were with the Queen, all the hairs on Sophie's back went up and she gave out a growl as he pushed past. She doesn't like him."

Sophie growled a bit at that. "See, she understands me." Eleanor looked at Sophie and gave her a hug. "I saw him talking to Eloise when we left the church too," added Eleanor. "I don't think she likes him much. She's been very quiet since."

"Of course, she's been quiet," said Harry. "She can't speak."

"You know what she means," said Grace. "I've noticed it too."

93

Harry didn't, but he wasn't going to argue any further now.

Eleanor carried on, "They were having a very heated conversation. At least, Guy of Caen was telling her something very aggressively. He was leaning right into to her and pointing at her. I think he understands some of her sign language too. She waved her arms about in reply and I thought that for a moment he was going to slap her, but he backed off and went away."

Just then, they jumped. A huge drum banged with a deep tone. Then another. Then another. The rhythm increased then settled down into a regular pattern.

Boom! Boom! Boom! Boom!

They glided silently out into the middle of the river and the children saw that oars were passed out through the side of the ship - twenty-five each side, they counted. There were three men to each oar at either side of the boat, each with bulging shoulders and arms. Although the ship had two masts for sails, it was being rowed down the river by the crew.

Boom! Boom! Boom! Boom!

The drums were used to keep all the rowers in time and they glided gently down the river towards the sea.

The Captain turned from his own place at the front of the poop deck and walked up to the children, paying them some proper attention for the first time. This time, his eyes did not dart everywhere. Instead, he watched the children carefully and intently.

"Well," the Captain said, "I have cabin boys in my charge, but few are as young as any of you, Master Harry. And I have given young girls from the royal household passage to Normandy and to Aquitaine, but I cannot say that I have ever been told to obey the orders of anyone of your age before. I hope you're going to prove that you are worth it." He looked at them with a certain amount of worry, but he spoke to them like adults not like children and it made them trust him rather more.

"Excuse me, Sir," asked Harry, thinking of the conversation that the three of them had just been having. "What do you know about Sir Guy of Caen?"

The Captain looked at Harry, wondering how best to answer him. "He's the King's agent and bears the King's signet ring to prove his authority. That should be enough. I wasn't expecting him, and if I'm honest I'm not sure about him. I tell you I would rather take orders from you three than from him." The Captain then looked at them as if he had taken them into his confidence a little too much. "But don't tell him I said that. I hope he will keep out of the way. I do not know his exact business other than the fact that he has been sent to keep an eye on us! Let's hope he is what he's meant to be and here to protect you and help you on our mission.

"Now, you must come to the chart room and we must plan our journey."

They went down the steep ladder to the main deck and into the dimly lit chart room. The constant rhythm of the drums echoed around them. Each boom thumped strongly and faded away until they could hear the water around the boat and the creaking of the woodwork. Then another 'boom' would come and disguise the little noises until the sound of the drum faded out again.

In the chart room, the Captain introduced them to someone he only referred to as the Sailing Master: he said was responsible, with him, for the navigation of the ship. There, the children told the Captain their mission. With as much confidence as they could muster, the children told them they must travel to Hell's Bay, to the edge of Hell, and make sure the dragons were subdued so that Edwin could reforge the Sword of State. The Captain and the Sailing Master stood in silence, digesting their fate, thinking they would rather fight their enemies on the opens seas than face dragons. The Captain mulled it over and said simply: "It is the Queen's order. Make a course for Hell's Bay, Mr Master." Then he made a face and added, "Just as soon as we've worked out where exactly it is. For now we head west."

As if to break the spell, the rhythm of the drums changed. There were four sharp beats and then silence as the oars were lifted from the water.

"I must go on deck," said the Captain. "We are nearly at the mouth of the river and the sails must be set."

He went out of the door. As he left, he turned to the children and said, "There can be no better ship for our journey. Her name is The Saint George. Go up to the bow and you will see our figurehead. We will be taking a dragon to meet dragons!"

15. The Storm

When they left the mouth of the River Axe, the sails were unfurled and began to fill with air. At the same time, the oars were drawn into the boat in perfect unison. As they passed the headland, the wind hit the sails and Sophie and the children were caught entirely by surprise. From being dead flat, the deck tipped at an angle. Instead of gliding smoothly along the calm of the river, the ship began to climb over the waves as well. Sophie scrambled with her feet to stay composed, but it was hopeless and she slid onto the bottom edge of the boat with her legs splayed around her. Every attempt to regain her composure failed, especially when Grace and Eleanor slid after her so that they all fell in a heap. Harry had somehow managed to grab the side of the boat to stay upright, but he was laughing so much at the other three, he was hard put to hold on.

Once the children untangled themselves, a hearty sailor showed them how to stand with their legs apart and bend their knees so they could balance with the movement of the ship. Even with four legs, Sophie struggled and decided that in the interests of gracefulness, she would curl up at the edge of the deck. It didn't stop her smiling though - or sliding all the way across the deck again when the ship suddenly tacked.

The children went to the front and saw the tail of the magnificent dragon figurehead at the bow. Then they climbed up onto the back of it as if they were on a fairground carousel and felt the green scales carved into the wood. They would need to be in the water at the front of the boat or on dry land to see the figurehead in all its glory, with gilded wooden flames coming out of its mouth. Riding the dragon, they watched the most glorious sunset before they climbed down and returned to the stern of the ship.

Then they saw the storm clouds gathering behind them in the east, huge grey clouds bubbling up from the horizon and pushing towards them. A nervous captain ordered everything to be stowed away. Oars were lashed down with rope and hatches battened down to stop water rushing into them. Until then, the novelty of sailing and the smooth passage with the wind on their port heel meant the ship was fairly comfortable, even if they did have trouble walking around. By the time they were back on the poop deck, the wind was beginning to whip around in an unpredictable way and at one moment Grace slipped headlong into the Sailing Master's stomach. That hardly winded him, but he was clearly in no mood for jokes, "You're to go to your cabin and stay there. It'll be safer, and this storm will be far worse before it's calm again. Now!"

By the time the girls reached the Captain's cabin, the colour had drained from their faces and they were both reminded of what it was like to be seasick. The rosy colour in their cheeks was replaced by a green tinge and their good humours vanished just as quickly. Eloise looked even worse than Grace and even poor Sophie curled up in a corner whimpering.

Grace said crossly, "Didn't Anwen give you something for this, healer?" The last word was emphasised just before she began to retch. "I think I'm going to be sick."

Eleanor didn't answer. She was already being sick, but there was a relief in being sick and she heard Grace and remembered she was right. She reached into her bag and found the strange leaves Anwen had given her. They looked a little like bay leaves. "Chew one if it's really bad," Anwen had said. Eleanor put one in her mouth and started chewing. She didn't exactly feel better, but all of a sudden she no longer felt as if she wanted to die. Then she handed one to Eloise and Grace and even tried to put one in Sophie's mouth, but Sophie just spat it out. "Chew!" she shouted, and opened her mouth to show them. They chewed. Then Eloise pointed at her and Grace said something, so quickly did the leaf have an effect at making them feel better, but she could not hear as the storm had become so wild. Eleanor realised soon enough what they meant as she saw the other girls' lips and teeth turn bright green.

They might have smiled at that, but suddenly the ship felt as if it was rising, rising, rising, like an aeroplane taking off; only to be thrown to the ground again, then diving far below. It was a helter-skelter without the fun. They were climbing massive waves before falling into a trough of water the other side.

Next door, Edwin and Harry dared not hang their

hammocks. Their heads would have been smashed against the wooden walls of the tiny cabin like conkers on strings. Instead they crammed themselves into a corner, backs against one wall, feet against another. That was how small the space was. They could see the seams of the wooden planks that made up the boat pull apart and then push back together.

"They should make boats of out iron," thought Edwin, his blacksmith's mind at work. "One day they must make boats out of iron."

They were all like that for what seemed like hours, but if Grace had had a chance to look at her watch - which she had steadfastly wound every day - she would have known it was only 20 minutes since they had been sent to the cabins. Then there was a thunderous crash and the ship swung round and round, plunging in a most unpredictable way. The girls did everything they could to stay still in the cabin.

Minutes later, the cabin door was thrown open. "You must come at once," shouted the Sailing Master at the top of his voice. "Come now and be saved!" He held out a rope and through the open door, they saw the top of the stern mast was broken clean off 10 feet above the deck. They saw Edwin and Harry at the base of the mast and saw that they were tied to it. At once, Eleanor and Grace thought of treachery, but the Sailing Master shouted, "It's the only way to avoid being swept overboard. When we're there, I'll tie myself as well. God help us all."

It was madness, but Grace and Eloise allowed the rope to be wrapped around their waists. Even Sophie had a rope around her. Then it was Eleanor's turn, but as the Sailing Master wrapped it around her, the wind shifted again and the rope flung itself out tight as a piece of steel scaffolding. Eleanor was thrown to the side of the ship and clung to the edge of the deck, screaming.

"Help! Help!" Even though they could all see Eleanor, the scream was very faint and the wind whipped away the words. Harry, Grace and Edwin were tearing at the ropes around their waists where they had been tied, but they couldn't move them or undo them. The knots had become soaked and the ropes tore at the skin on their fingers, making them sore and bleed. It was amazing that they could hear Eleanor at all. The wind was so strong around them that they could hardly hear themselves think.

The Sailing Master held on to the rope again to try and reach Eleanor. Then a gust came across the boat, and the wind turned the rope into a giant whip and threw him out to sea, never to be seen again.

"Help me!" cried Eleanor again. "I can't hold on."

Only Eloise managed to loosen the knot around her and she edged along the deck holding one end of a long piece of rope attached to what little remained of the mast. She reached Eleanor and grabbed a hand which gratefully wrapped around her own. The others were suddenly blinded by a squall of rain, so they couldn't see what happened next. The rain stung on their faces and they had to shut their eyes.

As Eloise held tight to Eleanor's hand, Guy of Caen crawled along the edge of the deck. His black cloak bellowed above and he gave the impression of a giant bat as the lightning started and lit the scene.

There was no way Eloise could signal or shout at Guy. Even with a tongue to speak, he would never have heard. She just hoped he would grab Eleanor's other hand.

Guy's cloak was finally whipped away by the wind, and he managed to stand upright. But instead of helping, he stamped on Eleanor's other hand so that she had to let go of the deck with a scream and only Eloise's feeble grasp was saving her from oblivion.

In spite of all the wind and rain, Eleanor could hear what Guy of Caen said to Eloise, "We must be rid of her! It is our duty to King Louis of France! Let her go."

Eloise shook her head and uttered a groan from the depths of her belly. A guttural, "Nooooooooo!" emerged from her mouth. With all her strength, she pulled Eleanor towards her. Then, she scratched at the eyes and face of Guy of Caen, drawing blood and making him stagger back to the edge. He regained his stance before wiping his face and looking angrily at the blood on his fingers.

Suddenly, the rain squall passed and the wind changed. Harry opened his eyes and saw the wind catch the rope Eloise was holding, with Eleanor now firmly in her arms. It was whipped up and the two of them lost their footing to become a gruesome pennant, flying in the wind right over the edge of the ship. Harry looked on helplessly.

16. The Navigator

Suddenly the ship tipped right back in the other direction and Harry was looking at the sky, his back tight to the mast. He saw everything in slow motion. The rope was straight above him. Eloise and Eleanor were both forced to let it go. Down they flew, their backs towards him. Suddenly Eleanor's body hit him and winded him, but he acted as a cushion and he had the presence of mind to grab hold of her. Edwin had Eloise and they tied them both to the mast, giving them temporary safety.

When Harry looked up out to the edge of the boat, Guy of Caen had vanished, presumably taken by the wind and drowned.

Eleanor opened her eyes and tried to think about what she had heard in the midst of her ordeal. It was impossible and despite the noise of the storm, the exhaustion of the adventure made her pass out into a restless and nightmarish sleep, with her head resting on Sophie. By morning, she had forgotten all about it.

Eleanor woke from the storm with Sophie licking her face. The rain was falling heavily now and it was pitch black all around. Eleanor licked her lips, but all she could taste was salt. Then the rainwater refreshed her lips. The touch of water was delicious. She was so thirsty. She needed more water, but where would it come from? That was when Eloise, who was tied next to her by the mast passed her a cloth. It had been torn from her voluminous robes, and she had wrung all the salt water out of it before letting it soak up the rainwater. On the other side of her, Harry, who had already had a drink, shouted: "Suck it! Suck out the water!" Then it was much better. Just those few delicious drops gave her back her energy and strength; the others had experienced the same. So Eleanor held the cloth up to the rain again to soak it through. This time she let Sophie suck in the water. Then, even with the strength from the drink of water, she lay down and slept again. This time there were just bad dreams.

When they all awoke, dawn was breaking. The sun was just peeping up in the east, though that could be the only indication of where they were. Then it vanished again behind dark clouds and the night returned for a moment. The clouds stayed to hide the sun, but the day gradually became lighter.

The ship was dipping and diving, out of control, but it did not seem to be in danger of sinking. Harry, Eleanor and Grace could make out figures on the deck. The Captain was moving around. There beside him was the diminutive figure of Edwin, hacking away at broken ropes and rigging with an axe nearly as tall as him in an effort to help make the ship work in some way again.

Harry suddenly realised he wanted desperately to be away from the ropes around him. He remembered the penknife he had put into his pocket just before he had gone to visit Great Uncle Jasper in his study. He hacked at the thick rope around his waist. The rope was made of hundreds of tiny pieces of twine wound together, and it seemed each one only gave way at a time. It was infuriating. Harry felt utterly trapped. Finally, it split. Then he was able to set Grace and Sophie free. By then, Edwin had managed to release himself and used an axe to break Eloise's bonds open with one blow. That annoyed Harry after all the work he had done with his penknife.

The Captain emerged from the hold and came running to see them. "Thank God you are all still alive. We've lost the Sailing Master and nearly half the crew. Those who are left and aren't injured must work all day if we're to survive the night."

Harry saw sailors toiling all around him. So much seemed broken. Barrels had broken free from their bindings against the side of the ship and had rolled across smashing everything in their way, spreading their contents aimlessly as they went. He thought they should do something to assist: "How can we help, sir?"

The Captain looked at them, three children and a mute maid. Instead of being sarcastic or telling them to go and stay out of the way, as a normal adult might, he took Harry's offer at face value.

"I can spare no men to check the stores until I know the ship is water-tight and there are no more leaks. We'll need food and water. There are injured men too who need help." All of the crew looked battered and bruised. Harry had sore ribs from where Eleanor had landed on him, but he was clearly in a much better state than many of the crew. Some of them had giant splinters in their legs and arms. Others were crushed and being laid out in a makeshift hospital amongst the wreckage. Even the fittest looking were bruised and battered.

Eleanor stepped forward and pulled Eloise with her. "We can do that, can't we? Let's hope my herbs are still here. My book is safe under these robes and was protected from the rain." She pulled it out of her pocket with some relief, unwrapping it.

"We have no idea where we might be," added the Captain. "Without some guidance, I don't know how we might get back home. I need to someone to discover what's left of the chart room and the compass box."

"We'll do that, sir," said Harry. "Come on navigator Grace. I think it's time we showed our worth."

The Captain could not be sure what Harry meant by 'navigator' Grace, but did not question it and said, "Thank you."

While Eleanor and Eloise went off towards the front of the boat, the bow, to find the injured and some supplies, Harry and Grace turned towards the stern, to look at what was left of the chart room and cabins. Before they did that, they went up to the poop deck to look for the compass box. They had seen it earlier in front of the great tiller that steered the boat, mounted on a pillar and protected from the elements. It had not been protected enough. It had gone.

Harry was distressed and said, "We'll never find our way now, not without a compass."

"Yes we will," said Grace confidently.

"How?" replied Harry.

Grace looked around. She was still nervous about being accused of being a magician or worse a witch. "Come down to the chart room and I'll show you."

So, this time, it was Grace's turn to lead Harry.

The chart room was in chaos. The chart table in the centre of the room had been bolted to the floor, but all the drawers were thrown open. The Captain's cot had been thrown across the room, and his spare clothes were all over the floor.

Harry smiled.

"What is it?" asked Grace.

"It looks just like your room at home that time we visited!"

"No it doesn't! Anyway, I've no one to help me tidy up at home and now you're going to help in here." She stuck her tongue out at him.

"Oh, all right," Harry answered. "Now what were you going to show me?"

Grace pulled the watch and chain from under her neck. First of all, she opened the watch. "I couldn't wind it up last night. I hope it still works."

She held the watch to her ear and gratefully heard the sound: "Tick, tock, tick, tock, tick, tock," before winding it carefully. "That's good."

"But how is a watch going to show us where to go?" asked Harry.

"Here's how." Grace opened the back of the golden pocket watch and held it in the palm of her hand. There, beautifully engraved with north, east, south and west around the side was a tiny compass.

"Now, if we can find some maps and my star chart, we can work out where to go. Easy!" she added confidently.

107

"Cool. You really are a navigator!"

Grace suddenly looked a little uncertain. Her eyes began to fill with tears. "I don't think I am," she said. "Do you think we'll ever get home?"

"Of course we will," he said cheerfully, but quite uncertain himself. He hugged her and then added, "Now shall we clear up?" knowing the best thing for both of them would be to be busy.

It took them three or four hours. Once Eloise came in and brought them a beaker of murky water and some very tough and salty meat to chew. But the salt in the meat made them want the water, however murky, and the meagre meal revived them. They wanted to ask how things were going, but of course they wouldn't understand the answer. In any case, Eloise did not hang around long enough.

After they'd finished tidying, the little chart room looked almost normal - except for the pile of the Captain's clothes on the cot. They both agreed it was not their job to clear up his clothes, however busy he was.

Then, they began to look at the charts. Some had great stains of water all over them, but others were quite clear. They looked different to any maps they had ever seen before. Even where places were marked that they recognised, the coastlines were different. Harry said they looked like Roman maps: all wobbly and wrong.

Eventually Grace said, "I think this is Cornwall on this one, with the sea all around, but the Scilly Isles aren't marked."

"The Scilly Isles?" asked Harry.

"Yes," said Grace. "I'm sure that's where Hell's Bay is."

Harry stared at some rough marks on the map. "Maybe

it's here."

"They just look like rocks."

"Well the whole place was covered in rocks, if you remember. The boats had to zigzag all over the place to get to the land at low tide."

"OK," said Harry. "If it is, how do we get to it?"

Grace was crestfallen again. "I don't know."

Then she added, "Why don't you look at your silly book." But she hit a nerve with Harry, who was beginning to think his book was rather silly. He bit his tongue and swallowed the sharp words he had been about to say.

Instead he reached into his pocket in the waxed jacket where his slim green book had been protected from the rain and the storm and said, "Let's both look at our books."

So they both placed their books on the chart table. Grace put the compass next to it and Harry asked a question. It was similar to a question he had asked before, but he thought he would try again. Harry didn't see why the book should answer differently this time, "How do we get to Hell's Bay?"

There was plenty of light to see by as Grace had opened the star chart.

The gothic writing on the page said, "Go outside, use your eyes and look for a false dawn at night." Cryptic as ever, but this was a new answer.

Then something else happened. It was as if an invisible hand was drawing. Slowly, ragged lines appeared and joined each other to form an island. Then another. Then more lines appeared and a funny symbol appeared like a little child drawing the sun with rays all round.

Harry was watching this when Grace said, "Harry. The stars

have changed. And the watch. The hands keep moving from one time to another. From the time now to half past nine."

Harry looked at the stars projected onto the ceiling and then at the watch. Then Grace looked at Harry's book. "It's a map," she said. "It's much better than these charts. And there's the volcano."

"How can you tell?" asked Harry.

"It's smoking," said Grace. "Volcanoes always smoke from the top of them."

Then Harry looked again, and saw that it really was smoking. The funny symbol had changed into a tiny little mountain climbing out of the page. "Our books are working together Grace. We should've known we need to act as a team. We're nearly there. We just need to think and work it out. What do you think we do next?"

Grace looked at Harry as if he was simple, "Come on, Harry. We 'go outside and use our eyes.' It's obvious. Your book told you."

17. Hell's Bay

"What are you doing?" asked Harry.

They had come up onto the deck and again they had used what was left of the old ship compass housing as a makeshift table. Grace was lying down on the deck looking at the sky. Sophie had trotted across to join them and lay next to Grace with her legs in the air, looking intently upwards as well.

"I'm trying to see the stars and work out how to use this all together now."

Harry looked at the sky. He couldn't see anything from the star chart there at all. It was quite unlike the effect indoors where the star book threw its light strongly on the ceiling. It was daylight and as far as Harry was concerned, they couldn't see a thing, which was probably just as well since they had both forgotten about avoiding showing off their magic books in front of the crew.

"I can't see anything at all," said Harry.

"I can," replied Grace, "but only just. Look - there's Sirius, the Dog Star. It's one of the brightest. We'll have to try again when it's dark." She stood up and they went to find the others.

During the time they had been clearing up the chart room, the rest of the ship had been busy. Things had been tied down properly and there was a sail on the remaining mast. Once again there was a man at the tiller, and the Captain was instructing the crew to set sail. Everyone was exhausted but the ship was seaworthy and could sail. Once again the movement of the ship became gracious, rather than sick-making.

The Captain gathered up the children and Edwin, and took them to the chart room. He would have asked Eloise as well, but she could not be seen.

"We're lucky to be alive. Thank you for all your help, but I must tell you our mission is at an end. Without a compass, we can do little other than navigate home. Since the wind blew us west, we'll turn back to find England, but that in itself will be difficult enough."

"We've come too far to fail now," said Edwin. "We must go on."

"It's not that I don't have the will to go on," said the Captain. "It's just that we can't navigate without a compass, especially to a place no one has heard of!" He was angry now, from exhaustion and from his own inability to achieve anything other than survival.

"It's time to show him, Grace. He needs to know and then we can work together again," said Harry.

Eleanor was looking at them both, but she guessed she knew it was time to trust the Captain with the knowledge of their books and nodded. Sophie made it clear she agreed too with a wag of her tail.

So Grace and Harry opened up their books and the Captain marvelled at them. He looked at the watch with the compass and said he had never seen such things before. "Where did they come from?" he asked.

The children looked at each other and Harry just said, "They were gifts."

"Well," said the Captain, "We must use them wisely." He put his thumb on the chart that showed Cornwall. I know of these rocky islands. All sailors avoid them. There's nothing useful there. The ground around is too shallow. There are just wrecks of those who've gone too close. But if we must go there, we must."

"That's better," grumbled Edwin. "Something positive."

"But how can we use the knowledge?" asked Grace.

"The Sailing Master would have been more use to us, but we can only mourn him," answered the Captain. "But here is a guess from watching the skies at night for 30 years. The stars move all the time, but at the same time every day the same stars appear in the same place. Your magic clock shows two different times. What if one of them gives the time and the star chart gives the map of the sky at that time at the place of our destination. It would be powerful magic indeed. The problem will be how to use that knowledge."

"I think you're right," said Grace, suddenly excited, "And I know how to do it. We need to take the book outside and try to make the stars on the book match up with the stars in the sky and sail in the right direction. If the time on the watch matches with the real time, and the stars match we'll be in the right place. But it'll need to be dark. And we can use the compass to go in the right direction."

The Captain nodded, thinking it through. "That might work, but I still worry about the rocks and how we avoid them. And we must pray for a clear night so that we can see the real stars."

He looked round. "We must warn the crew of this magic. It'll frighten them otherwise. In the meantime, we use your compass and sail back east."

Eloise slipped back into the room. She looked anxious. Eleanor asked where she had been but she just shook her head, pointed out of the door and shrugged her shoulders in a meaningless way.

Night fell just after five o'clock. The waves were calm and their prayers seemed to be answered. The sky was crystal clear and the stars twinkled. The moon was bright too, so the chart, the books and the watch could be laid out again on the makeshift compass box and seen clearly. Then Grace opened the star book. Suddenly it was like looking at the sky with double vision. Grace and the Captain smiled at each other. The Captain shouted orders for a new course. The great tiller swung over. Almost imperceptibly, the real stars and the projected stars started to move together. As the stars and the watch moved on, they held their course on the same compass setting, getting closer and closer to Hell's Bay.

It was just after 9 pm when the lookout at the top of the mast shouted. "Daybreak. The Sun rises!"

"Relieve that man," shouted the Captain. "It cannot be daybreak." Then he turned to the gathering on the poop deck. "He's been confused by your magic," he said to the children. And he laughed with a worried look on his face.

But Harry stopped him. "No. He isn't confused. Remember

114

my book said: *Look for a false dawn at night.* This must be it. He must be seeing the glow from the volcano. That's what it meant. We're nearly there."

"Then we'll rest here tonight and recover ourselves," said the Captain. "I for one wish to approach the edge of Hell after the real daybreak, when we can see the rocks and face the dangers in the light."

18. Volcano's Edge

Boom! Boom! Boom! Boom!

The children all woke to the sound of drums. The deck was absolutely level and the children leapt up to go and see what was happening. The children wrapped their coats and cloaks around them quickly, and went out onto the deck. The beautiful crisp clear evening had led to heavy frosts. On the forward mast, the sail hung loosely, but was stiff with frost. The sea around about was flat with barely a ripple. Although it was freezing, without wind on their faces, no one felt that cold.

The crew was short of men after losing so many to the storm. But in spite of that, the Captain had enough men to row with 15 oars on each side.

"Look," said Harry, pointing to the front. There, a single plume of smoke rose high into the sky, untouched by wind until it was as tall as a skyscraper. Even then the smoke just drifted gently to the west. "There's our dragons' lair. Well done

116

Grace for getting us here."

Behind them, Edwin had manned the drums. He was too short to row, although plenty strong enough. Instead, he had been put in charge of the rhythm of the boat. But when the children spotted him, all they could see was his hair peeking over the top of the huge drums, even though he stood on a platform. The girls giggled uncontrollably at the sight, but Harry just about contained himself and said: "What do you think of your furnace, Edwin?"

There was a slight change in the rhythm of the drums, but all Edwin managed to say was "Humph!" before the beat became normal again.

The Captain came towards them. "It will take almost all of the morning to reach the island, and then I'll need your help. You'll need to sit on the bowsprit and look into the water for rocks. There will be a man with a line and a lead - a long rope we use to measure the depth - but you must shout out if you see rocks. The water will be clear enough, I hope."

"What's the bowsprit," asked Grace, sensibly enough, since none of them knew.

"It's where our own dragon is fitted, the figurehead at the bow you sat on before the storm. Now, go and have your breakfast so you're ready."

The change in the weather was good for everyone and the children had slept all night. Now they were refreshed for the next stage of the adventure. They gathered in the chart room for breakfast, where Harry and Grace noticed, slightly guiltily, that the Captain's clothes had been cleared away. Eloise indicated she would get their food for them and went off to the stores, while the children chatted and talked more about the Prophecy.

Harry quoted from the Prophecy:

"Hell's Bay will sound with clashing tones."

"I think that bit's easy now," said Eleanor. "Edwin is going to forge a new Sword and have you seen all his hammers and tools? I bet he makes a lot of noise. Or maybe it's the drums."

"What worries me is how we're going to get the diamond the Queen talked about that the dragons are hoarding. The Prophecy doesn't even mention a diamond but just talks about an oily stone. It's a bit different," added Harry, "and it seems we can't kill the dragons. Do they sleep at all? Can we tip-toe into their cave?"

None of them had answers to that yet.

"Read the bit about Dragons' Bane," said Eleanor. "I've been thinking about how we might use it. If we can find it."

"By Dragons' Bane, the children three
Will dull and lull the putrid lair,
To pluck from him the oily stone
By breathing out the vapoured air."

They were silent. Then Grace said, "Ask your book, Harry."

So Harry opened up an empty page and asked the question, "How do we get into the dragons' lair?"

The tiny gothic script wrote in the centre of the page:

"Think like a beekeeper." That certainly made them all stop and think.

"I had a bee sting last year," said Eleanor. "Do you remember? We stumbled across their nest in the garden and it swelled up on my arm. It really hurt and then itched for days."

"Well, I think dragons might sting just a little bit more," answered Harry, shuddering.

"Well yes," said Eleanor. "But don't you remember? Mummy and Daddy had the nest moved. The man came in his silly clothes. That big white hat with the net."

Grace always felt a bit forlorn when Harry and Eleanor talked about their parents, but she tried not to show it. "Where are you going with this?"

Eleanor was excited. "I think I understand it. He had a machine that produced smoke and all the bees got sleepy so he could go near them. But he didn't have to kill the bees. He smoked them out. It's what we have to do with the dragons: we must *dull and lull the putrid lair... by breathing out the vapoured air*. We have to burn Dragons' Bane to make smoke, don't you see?"

"I think so," said Harry, concerned enough at the thought of even going near sleepy bees, let alone dragons. "But won't it send us to sleep too?"

"I don't think it will. We've already smelt Dragons' Bane in the carriage. We hated the smell, but it didn't make us sleep, did it? In fact, it woke us up."

"You're right," said Harry. "Now we need to work out how to make it all work. Where's Eloise anyway? I'm hungry. She can't have spent this long just getting breakfast."

Eleanor got up to look, but suddenly Eloise came bustling in and they devoured all the food quickly, ready for the day ahead.

On the deck, the islands were much closer. The children were sent ahead to sit on the figurehead and slowly the ship edged closer and closer to their destination. Once or twice, the children shouted for rocks and they suddenly swerved as the tiller was moved across. The man with the line swung it over his head so that it splashed into the water far ahead of them. The lead weight made it sink down to the bottom. As the boat moved over it, he could measure the depth before doing the whole thing again. In doing this, the poor sailor became thoroughly soaked and must have been freezing, but he never complained. The seabed came closer and closer to the bottom of the boat. Edwin slowed the drums and they anchored, waiting briefly whilst the gig, a shallow rowing boat, was put into the water to explore further. Harry wished that he had his binoculars, but it was too bad. He could picture them hanging on the hook on the back of his door in his bedroom at Great Uncle Jasper's house.

Then Edwin was calling. They gathered together to go down into the boat to explore.

"Is it safe?" asked Grace. Edwin looked at her sharply. "Of course it isn't safe. There be dragons here, but dragons sleep during the day. Unless you go into their lair and stir them up like bees, they won't know we're here until it's dark. By then, we'll hide aboard the boat and stay silent until dawn so they don't notice us."

"My tools are packed in the boat. We must go and find the volcanic flow for my furnace. Then I'll forge anew the Sword of State with the shattered parts of Ascalon!" Edwin glowed with the pride thinking of the work he was going to have to do. "Come on!"

As they edged into the bay, Harry talked to Edwin about what they had worked out and he nodded, listening carefully. "I can forge the Sword," said Edwin, "but you must find me that diamond for the handle."

Harry asked, "But we don't understand. The Queen and

you are both talking about diamonds, but the Prophecy talks about an oily stone. Surely they are different?"

"Diamonds are rare things, Harry," replied Edwin. "Diamonds were made when the earth was formed and the heat was greater than even the volcano's lava we'll find today. I've only seen a handful of these small stones in my life. They are precious, but once I went to the King's jeweller to fetch a diamond for the dagger your sister wears and I picked up a pretty pebble. It was much larger than the shiny diamonds in the workshop, but still only the size of my thumb. It never glittered like a diamond, but it had a gleam, an oily glimmer that caught my eye. I asked the jeweller what it was and he replied, 'That, Master Edwin, is the largest diamond I've ever had in this workshop and I must cut it. Put it down now, for it's worth more than both our lives.' That is your oily stone. I watched that master of his craft cut that diamond into what you and I understand, but before his magic was worked upon it, it just looked like an oily stone. A pretty pebble, mind you, but an oily stone. That's what you'll be looking for. And if the king of the dragons is hoarding it, it will be neither small nor easy to get hold of."

Everyone looked with wonder at the island they were approaching. There was a long beach. It was not golden sand, but a beach of grey ash, interrupted by lengthy almost imperceptibly slow streams of orange lava, which changed in colour and turned into dark brown rock where they hit the sea. At these points, the sea steamed like a kettle that had just boiled. There was no greenery at all at the water's edge, but Eleanor shouted, "Look up! Look up at the hill!"

The hill was like an extraordinary stripy baggy jumper;

the sort of jumper that might have been sent to one of the children by a great aunt and which they would have refused to wear except by force. Orange stripes of lava ran downwards. Each of these was edged with grey ash and brown rock where nothing grew. Then in between were great wide stripes of purple flowers, growing in a place where nothing should grow at all.

"It's Dragons' Bane," said Eleanor. "We've found it. We're on the right track, at last!"

A sailor jumped over the bow as they neared the beach. He turned and grinned. "It's warm," he said, "beautifully warm." Harry noticed it was the sailor who had been so wet with the measuring line and was glad to think that he at least might be warmed up.

Then activity broke out everywhere. The Captain directed a team to go with Eleanor and Grace to gather up the flowers, as many as possible. Sophie followed gently with them, gingerly picking her way across the land making sure her sensitive paws did not become burned by the hot ash. Eloise followed carrying a large basket, which she placed on her head.

Another team helped Edwin unpack his tools and lug them towards the stream of lava so that he could begin to forge the Sword. The lava would be his furnace to melt and forge the pig iron that would be turned into a blade and handle for the new Sword of State. There was no need to gather firewood, which was good, for nothing grew on that island except the purple flowers. He nursed the plain metal box that held the splinters from Ascalon. When he opened it, here at the foot of the dragon's volcano, he saw each them glowed more fiercely than he had ever seen before.

Once orders were given by the Captain, he and Harry boarded the gig again with the remaining sailors left to row it.

Their mission was the most dangerous. They must find the dragons' lair.

19. Nightmare

There was no drum in the little gig to count the measure of the oars, but the Captain sat by the tiller and acted as his own coxswain. "One, two... one, two," he muttered to set the pace, but these were the most experienced of the sailors and that was enough. It was a gentle pace and the boat was infinitely more manageable than the great flagship, The Saint George. Harry knelt in the bow. This time, he was not looking for rocks. There was a sailor with that duty lying next to him. He was looking for the dragons' lair, eyes searching from side to side, carefully seeking out any signs. Once again, he was cross with himself for leaving the binoculars behind, and swore that he would always keep them in his coat pocket when he got back home. If he got back home.

The afternoon wore on and they reached the northernmost point of the channel between the two islands then turned back again. Nothing. No caves, no smoke, no dragons. Surely they were in the right place? They rounded the point on the last stretch back towards the beach.

Suddenly there was a fierce clash, metal upon metal. Harry stood up and listened.

Clang, clang, clang! Clang, clang, clang! Clang, clang, clang! Then it stopped.

"Is that a sword fight I hear?" muttered the Captain to himself. Then loudly to his sailors, "Keep steady."

Then it started again.

Clang, clang, clang! Clang, clang, clang!

"It's Edwin," said Harry with a smile and relief in his words. "*Hell's Bay will sound with clashing tones*, he quoted. It's not a fight, but the Sword being made."

Then he suddenly stared into the steep cliff, the one he had stared at so carefully on the way out. "Here! Turn towards the cliff." There was a tiny gap just above the sea level. "It's a cave."

The Captain directed the gig towards the cliff.

"Stop!" This time the sailors backed their oars at the shout, and Harry fell back down with a thump. It was the sailor looking out for rocks who had shouted, "There be rocks. We'll have to go to the port, then starboard then port again to be clear." So they zigzagged their way across to the cliff.

"*Beware the direct route*," said Harry to no one in particular. "This must be it."

As they approached the cave, slowly, gently, the opening got bigger and bigger.

"Easy oars," was the command this time and the sailors just lifted their oars out of the water. As they move slowly towards the entrance there was just room for the boat to glide inwards towards the gloom.

Harry clambered back and sat next to the Captain. "Surely

this is a magical cave, the way the entrance got bigger as we got closer."

The Captain smiled. "Magical it may be, Harry. But 'tis the tide that makes the cave bigger. The level of the sea is dropping and later tonight this entrance will be hidden again."

Harry kicked himself for being so foolish, and was glad the Captain had not teased him about it, but there was no time to worry about that.

Inside was bigger, much, much bigger, with a high ceiling arching way above the water. They should have been in darkness. Yet within was a luminous glow that lit a grand cavern. Two channels of lava slowly fed their molten rock into the sea either side of them, but there was more to the glow than even that. Two or three hundred yards beyond they could see sleeping dragons on the rocks, motionless, but snoring. As they snored little trickles of flame flew out of their mouths, creating more light within.

The light might have been pretty, but the smell was not. If you imagine a kennel without a window full of dogs, all with bad breath, combined with the smell of a hundred dead and rotting rats, then this was all that and much worse. Much, much worse. "Putrid." said Harry to himself. "Now I know what it means." He thought it was just about possible that Dragons' Bane smelt better than this.

The sailors themselves were almost paralysed with fear, but the Captain steadied them with a whisper and discipline stayed firm. The Captain said to Harry. "Remember now, this is no time for heroics. For now we're here to look."

At that moment, the largest dragon seemed to open one eye and stare directly at them. An extra large jet of flame blew out of his nostrils and they saw clearly where he was lying. He was perched on a rock in the centre of the cavern, but this was no ordinary rock. This was a rock made of gold and silver and gemstones. It glittered brilliantly and threw patterns across the wall. The crew of the boat sat motionless, mesmerised by the single eye of the dragon, convinced that soon they would be burnt to a cinder and torn into pieces when it woke.

The dragon lifted a paw and scratched its nose. Then the eye shut and the flames subsided. The dragon had not seen them. It was still sleeping.

Quietly and quickly, the Captain gave the command to row and the boat turned back into the sunlight and they went back to the beach. They were all delighted their trip to the dragons' lair was over and they all hoped they would not have to go back. Except Harry. He knew he had to go back. And the oily stone would be under the largest dragon on the little island made of treasure.

As they returned to the beach, they saw the girls waiting with great mounds of purple flowers. The sun was dipping down in the west and they could see Edwin silhouetted with his hands in the air. Harry could not quite make out why. Then as they came closer, he realised. Edwin was holding up the new Sword. Its point was resting on the ashen beach. His hands were on the hilt, but since it was much taller than him, his hands were above his head.

"The Sword is forged," said Edwin once they were on the beach. It was tall with a wide flat blade and simple metal hilt and hand guard. "The blade needs sharpening and finishing. Its power will be complete only when the diamond is fitted here." He pointed to a delicate iron cage at the top of the hilt.

"Later, I'll add ornate work in gold so that it looks special at ceremonies. But once the stone is fitted, it should have all the power of Ascalon. For now, we must return to the ship before darkness descends and the dragons awake. You have taken your time!"

Later, the ship was shrouded in darkness and the men aboard were given orders to be silent for fear of rousing the dragons. There was little risk of those orders being broken. Inside the chart room, Ascalon, re-forged, sat on the table and the green light of the blade glowed within. The Captain, the children, Edwin and Eloise sat round in council, making plans for the next day.

Harry described the dragons' lair and what they had seen. "I don't want to go back there, but I must. It stinks, it's dark and the dragons look more evil than I could have imagined. The dragons were asleep, but it seems clear they're easily disturbed. We will definitely need the Dragons' Bane, Eleanor."

"We started to experiment on the beach," replied Eleanor. "We dried some out in the heat of the lava, and then set fire to it. It certainly burnt and there was a terrible smell, but it burnt so quickly. I don't know how to keep it burning for the time you need to row and get the diamond."

"Time," added the Captain, "is something you don't have. We only spotted the cave as the tide was going out late in the afternoon. The cave won't be uncovered until the afternoon. Today, we only went to the entrance and returned to the ship just in time for darkness to fall. Tomorrow you'll have less than an hour. You'll need to be swift."

With a grim reality, Edwin added, "If we survive the night with the dragons awake. Each hour of the darkness will be more dangerous than the one before."

Harry opened his book and kept asking it questions whilst the others talked through what they would need the next day. Harry's book just kept writing out the Prophecy again and again. He slammed it shut.

"Impatience won't help you, Harry. The book's meant to help you. Read out the Prophecy again. Aloud, so we all may hear," Edwin commanded.

So Harry did. And they sat silently, wondering about its cryptic words. All of them, that is, except Edwin, who fumbled around under his leather apron to find something. When he had found it, he placed it on the table. "This is one thing that will help."

It was his pipe. Harry petulantly said, "Smoking that may help you relax, but I don't know what good it will do us!"

"Think again, Harry" said Edwin. Harry felt he was being put down unreasonably. After all, it was he who would have to face the danger.

Eleanor worked it out as well and came to Harry's rescue. "Of course! You'll have to smoke it!"

"Oh," said Harry. "I see." Then so did Grace.

"Will someone explain?" asked the Captain, who had never seen a pipe before and had no idea what this object was.

"Show him," answered Harry. So Edwin lit the pipe and puffed away. Then he drew in the smoke and blew it towards the Captain, who spluttered.

"You see," said Harry. *"By breathing out the vapoured air."*

The Captain looked in amazement. "You do that by choice?" he asked, but Edwin ignored him.

He passed the pipe across to Harry, "I think you'd better

practice young Harry, otherwise it is you who will be spluttering to wake the dragons - and Dragons' Bane won't be nearly as sweet as these herbs." So Harry puffed and choked, and puffed and choked, and eventually got the hang of holding enough smoke to breathe it out, before turning green, feeling sick and saying, "I never, ever want to smoke again."

"Very wise," muttered the Captain.

While he did that, the others went through the plans until Grace suddenly said, "I've been thinking about why the dragon couldn't see you with the eye he opened. That eye must be blind. *Beware the direct route* isn't about zigzagging to miss the rocks. It means go towards the dragon's blind side. And *wear another's suit* isn't about that hairy tweed suit Horrible Hair Bun made you wear at all. I know what you have to do." So Grace explained it. Then the Captain told them to go to bed and get some sleep. There was work to be done in the morning.

The worry should have kept them all awake, but all the exercise and energy spent during the day meant the girls soon dozed off. Harry was less fortunate. It must have been two in the morning when he heard the noise.

"Help me! I can't hold on." It was Eleanor's voice. He rushed into the girls' room with Edwin close behind him holding an axe, but it was put down quickly. Eleanor was having a nightmare and Eloise was gently stroking her head. The screams changed into gibberish and she seemed to go to sleep again. Then quite suddenly, she sat up with her eyes wide open and shouted, "We must be rid of her! It is our duty to King Louis of France! Let her go." But she was still asleep and collapsed back. With those words, Eloise had shrunk back. But no one noticed, for both Grace and Harry were tucking Eleanor back into her cot. Harry said, "Mummy always says not to wake her when she dreams. It will be fine in the morning, I hope."

"We must discover what that means," said Edwin. "Where can she have had that idea or heard those words? And why hasn't she mentioned it before? King Louis of France is England's worst enemy. Treachery is near and we must watch our backs!" Only at the last moment did Edwin stop himself from thumping the side of the cot, realising what a noise he might make. Instead, he smashed his bunched fist into his other hand.

"I'll stay here with the girls," said Edwin. "Harry, return to the other cabin and sleep." Edwin stayed and watched over them. Sophie whined once gently and lay right next to Eleanor's cot, her eyes moving from Eleanor to Edwin to Eloise, watching carefully. Like the others, she was confused as to where the traitor might be. Her sixth sense was faulty and since Guy of Caen had vanished, she too was struggling to think where the traitor could be found.

Harry could not sleep, of course. He thought about the following day and wondered what on earth Eleanor had meant. It would have to wait until morning.

20. Treachery

Harry's 'suit' had to be prepared for his adventure into the dragons' lair. It was a brilliant piece of thinking by Grace, but the carpenters had their work cut out. They started before sunrise, just as dawn was breaking with a glimmer of light enabling them to see what they were doing. Ropes had been drawn from the stores in the hold. Pulleys were set up. A makeshift crane was established over the bow. Finally, everything was in place to move the figurehead from the bowsprit. The saw rasped its way backwards and forwards through the old oak. The Saint George, the flagship of the King's fleet, was to lose her figurehead and instead it was to be fitted to the gig and become a disguise for Harry.

Once the figurehead was lifted, the carpenters needed to hollow it out. The solid piece of oak from which it was fashioned had hardened and there was neither room nor time to spare. Finally there was space enough for a small boy to crawl inside. But he needed to see, so an eye was drilled out.

It was tunnel vision but it would have to do. Then a hollow needed to be made in the mouth. This dragon disguise would not make real flames, but it would blow real smoke.

Once this was done, fitting the figurehead, Harry's new 'suit', to the gig was easy. Making the gig float was not. Great empty barrels were tied to the bow of the gig so that the weight of the figurehead did not drown it. Then it floated, but it became a beast to row, especially since there was now only room for two oarsmen as well as Harry and Edwin, who had insisted on going. "Someone experienced with a pipe must accompany him!" he said, with a grim smile on his face.

It was not until the afternoon that Harry and Grace were able to find time alone with Eleanor and ask the question that had been in their minds all morning. Several times Harry had attempted to begin the conversation with Eleanor, but someone always interrupted them. Even Eleanor brushed Harry and Grace away, saying she needed to prepare the Dragons' Bane properly to make it work in the pipe. Periodically that morning a foul smell wafted across the boat as she experimented on the poop deck.

Finally, just as everything was ready for the expedition, Harry was able to ask the question, "What did you mean last night in your nightmare?"

"What nightmare?" replied Eleanor looking at them weirdly.

"Don't you remember?" said Harry. "You were crying out for help."

"Yes," said Grace. "You said, 'You must be rid of her. It is our duty to King Louis of France!'"

Eleanor looked at them each slowly, and then put her hand

to her mouth. "That wasn't last night. And I'd completely forgotten about it. The horrors of the storm must have hidden it in my mind. But it wasn't me who said it."

"But you said it last night," interrupted Grace.

"Never mind," said Harry. "Let her speak."

"It was in the storm. It was Guy of Caen." Eleanor paused. "I remember now. He trod on my hand and shouted that instruction to Eloise. Then something happened and he vanished. He was one of the ones drowned. He was the traitor. We never did like the look of him."

They all looked at each other aghast. "But that means Eloise is a traitor as well." said Harry.

"But she saved my life," said Eleanor remembering more. "She scratched at his eyes and made him bleed. That's why he went overboard. It doesn't make sense. Why would she save me if she was a traitor?"

The question went unanswered. Edwin and the Captain came up to the children.

"It is time, Harry." said the Captain. "Are you ready?"

Harry looked at them with a moment of panic, driving the conversation that he had just been having out of his mind. "No. I don't think I'll ever be ready."

Edwin looked at him. "Then you are honest and you're a real man. You cannot be ready until you look your fears in the eye. So you must *box up your fears and frights* just as St George did and you'll succeed. The boat is ready."

Eleanor unbuckled the girdle around her waist, the belt which bore the short dagger that Edgar the Librarian had given her. "Here, Harry," she said. "Take this with you. You may need it to help you."

Harry reached out to take the dagger, but then he paused. "No, Eleanor. It was a gift for you for your own defence. Who knows, you may need it yourself here. Look out for each other. We have axes and cutlasses in the boat if we need them."

"Hurry please," said the Captain, "or you'll miss the tide!"

So they had left the flagship, climbing down into the odd-looking little boat, a dragon at the front, a gig at the back and two barrels strapped to the side.

At that stage, a gentle southerly breeze started to blow, helping the oarsmen by pushing the cumbersome craft towards the island and the dragons' lair quickly. Everyone on The Saint George watched until the strange gig turned the headland and went out of sight.

Eleanor had Sophie by her side and looked at Grace, "We must find Eloise and ask for an explanation. I don't understand it and it's hard to believe. Maybe I misheard in the storm."

"Do you think we should ask the Captain to help us?" replied Grace.

"No," said Eleanor. "There might be nothing to it. If it were Guy of Caen we had to face, then certainly, but Eloise is timid. In any case, we have Sophie with us and I have my dagger."

"I agree then," said Grace.

The girls went to the stern of the ship and the cabins, where they expected to find Eloise. Outside Edwin and Harry's door, Sophie's hackles rose and she started to growl. It was a warning sign.

"Where are the guards?" asked Grace. Two sailors should have been standing outside the door of the cabin, where the Sword of State was stored.

Very gingerly, Eleanor pushed open the door of their cabin

and the three of them walked slowly in. A strange green glow lit the room. Eloise was standing by the long window at the back of the cabin. She shook her head from side to side as if to say, "No," but it was too late. The door was slammed shut and the girls and Sophie found themselves staring at the face of Guy of Caen, who was holding the Sword of State towards them. It glowed brightly in his hand.

The heat and stink of his fetid breath was felt on their cheeks as he leant in and hissed, "I'm so glad you're here. I can deal with you once and for all as well as this Sword."

Eleanor was shocked, but managed to speak up, "How did you survive?"

"Your friend Eloise fed me and cared for me - just at the moment when she thought she might be rid of me too. I hid in the hold waiting for my moment. I bet you didn't expect that! She's been in my power these last six months while my true sovereign, the King of France has had her brother locked up in his dungeon."

"Eloise!" said Eleanor looking up at her, but the girl only looked shamefully at the floor.

"Enough," said Guy of Caen. "Eloise, break open that window!"

Eloise broke the long gallery window at the back of the ship. Then with one broad step, he turned and flung the Sword out of the window.

Sophie had been waiting for her chance and saw it now, during the brief moment he had his back turned. She pounced and knocking him over, she bit the traitor hard on the shoulder. Then with a single leap, she flew out of window into the sea after the Sword.

Eleanor took her chance and drew her dagger, wishing she really knew how to use it. Its blade now glowed intently as she pointed it at the neck of the traitor on the floor. Eloise had shrunk back against the wall of the cabin, inert. Grace was by the window looking into the sea and threw off her cloak. She was a good swimmer, but it would be freezing and frightening. She turned back towards Eleanor and looked at her.

"Go!" Eleanor shouted. And with that encouragement, Grace dived into the sea after the dog and the Sword, but not without crying "Help!" at the top of her voice.

Inside the cabin, Guy recovered his breath and looked at the dagger and Eleanor. "Don't think two children will stop me!" He was fit and a warrior. The bite did little to stop him and with a swift move, he knocked the dagger out of Eleanor's hand so that it skidded across the floor to Eloise's feet. Now Guy of Caen had Eleanor in a neck lock.

"Pick up the dagger, girl!" hissed Guy to Eloise. "At least that's got rid of that ridiculous dog and one of the children. Now come here. Finish the job and I'll see to it that your brother is freed."

Eloise came towards Eleanor looking her straight in the eye, with the dagger drawn. But Eleanor noticed as she did so, she shook her head almost imperceptibly. A signal to Eleanor. Eleanor picked up her leg and scraped the sole of her shoes hard down Guy's shin onto his foot. He released his grip and Eleanor threw herself out of the way, just enough for Eloise to push the dagger into his stomach, wound him and put him out of action.

That wasn't the end of it though. Eloise turned the dagger to herself, looking at Eleanor and mouthing the words, "I'm sorry." She was about to kill herself to escape the guilt of it all. But the door was broken down by the Captain and the sailors who overpowered both the traitors.

Outside the boat, the water was clear. Once she had recovered from the shock of the cold, which was like someone punching her in the stomach, Grace could see right down to the shallow bottom. She hated swimming without goggles and the salt water stung her eyes, but she ignored it and dived deeper. Below her, she could see Sophie struggling to pull the Sword from the sandy seabed with her mouth. It was cutting into her gums and jaw before she managed to gain a grip on its hilt and pull it up towards the surface and Grace. When they reached the surface, breathing air back into their lungs was a relief. Sophie drew the air deeply through her nose, resolutely holding onto the hilt, whilst Grace shivered, teeth chattering and lips turning blue.

A boat had been launched to rescue them. It was only just in time to save them both from the cold and from sinking back under the waves.

21. Dragons' Lair

Harry and Edwin knew nothing about the events on The Saint George. Once at the entrance of the cavern, Edwin and the oarsmen swapped places. Edwin would row now, whilst the two oarsmen were to leap out of the boat with a brazier each. These were full of Dragons' Bane and would be lit from the lava and then tended by the sailors. Meanwhile, Harry and Edwin would go into the centre of the cavern, to the island made of treasure, guarded by the oldest and largest of the dragons.

Whilst the sailors lit the braziers, Edwin lit up the pipe full of the Dragons' Bane as well. The putrid stench of the lair and the revolting flowers combined into a really nauseous smell, but the four of them carried on with their work, ignoring it as far as possible.

Edwin rowed slowly and steered with the oars. Harry whispered instructions to him from his strange position scrunched up inside the hollow in the figurehead. They went round the left-hand side of the water, so that their disguised boat would come towards what they hoped was the dragon's blind eye. As they closed in, Harry puffed on the pipe, wanting to gag all the time and blew the smoke through the wooden figurehead's nostrils. A trickle of smoke headed towards the dragon. Harry could see the smoke being drawn into the dragon's nostrils, and then suddenly the creature lifted its head and a great rush of flame roared out of his mouth. The flames engulfed the little boat and waves rocked it. It was a dragon sneeze! Both Harry and Edwin were protected from the flames by the figurehead, and they held their breath. The dragon settled its head down again and Harry indicated to Edwin to pull forward, quite unable to stop his hand shaking as he did so.

"I can't see the oily stone," whispered Harry. Then he made a brave decision. "I've got to get out. Keep smoking," he told Edwin, passing him the pipe. Now Edwin had to manage two oars and the pipe. Even so, he reached out to make sure an axe was within easy reach. Harry slipped over the side and with some relief found the water was not only warm, but shallow. It was not rock though. The island was built of treasure and as Harry crept out of the water, gold and silver flagons studded with jewels shifted beneath his feet and caused him to trip. Clattering of metal on metal echoed throughout the cavern. Harry froze.

Then the dragon opened his eye. It was looking straight at him and Harry prayed it really was blind.

Suddenly, the dragon lifted its paw and scratched its nose, just as it had the night before. Then Harry saw the stone. The dragon had covered it with his paw. Harry took his chance and grabbed it, crouching back down as he did so and slipping it into his jacket pocket.

The dragon put its paw back down, and Harry slowly crept backwards. But suddenly the dragon was groping around, sleepily. It knew the diamond was gone! Edwin blew another puff of smoke, but even in its sleep the dragon was angry and instinctively felt what was happening. Even the Dragons' Bane could not keep the animal's subconscious greed from working, and it lashed out its paw. An angry claw went right through Harry's tweed jacket and sleeve, where it struck his skin and wounded him. Harry cried out and bit his tongue to try and stop the noise, but the pain was agony. Then the dragon couldn't get its claw out and started to wave Harry's arm around.

Edwin was out of the boat in an instant with his axe, pipe in mouth, puffing away and chanced his moment. With a sudden crash, he cut off the dragons' long toe with one blow and shouted, "Go!" Harry made it to the edge of the boat. In spite of the pain the injury must have caused the dragon, the extra smoke must have lulled it like an anaesthetic. It lay down to sleep again. But Harry was feeling so sleepy as well. One hand slipped off the side of the boat, and then the other, and he sank down under the water. Edwin grabbed the collar of his coat, picking him up by his neck like a small puppy, and threw him into an uncomfortable heap on the decking boards.

Harry's scream of pain and Edwin's shout must have been heard. The cave began to fill with a shuffling noise as other dragons began to stir in their sleep.

There was no way Edwin could tend to Harry now. They must get out of there. He turned the boat as quickly as possible and rowed furiously, collecting the other two sailors on the way. Outside, the fresh air was like a tonic but now the rowers had to fight against the waves.

When they were half way towards The Saint George, the volcano started spewing.

"Those be angry dragons," said Edwin. Then loudly, "Pull hard!" As if the oarsmen needed more encouragement.

Grace was watching the volcano from the poop deck of the flagship with the Captain. She was wrapped in her own heavy furs, with another borrowed cloak that was far too large spread all around her on the floor. Her teeth were still chattering from her swim and she wondered if she would ever be warm again. Darkness had fallen only minutes earlier as the clouds were gathering and the wind began to strengthen. It was blowing from the south and whipping up the waves. If they had not been so worried, what they saw might have been a marvellous spectacle. Sparks flew from the volcano, and then great fountains of light glowed and spat like Roman candles. It was a magnificent, spontaneous fireworks display.

This was a display with a difference. Dragons flew in and out of the sparks. They circled the mountain blowing great streams of flames from their mouths. They dived down into the very centre of the volcano before more flew out, with others coming from the side. This was a not a nest of angry bees, nor even a nest of angry hornets. These were angry dragons stirred and waking from their sleep, gathering their strength.

Down below, Eleanor was tending to an injured Sophie. Guy of Caen and Eloise were in the hold, clapped in irons, prisoners and traitors.

For now, the worry was Harry. Peering down onto the

roughening sea, Grace and the Captain could see the gig making its way as fast as possible back towards the boat, but no one could know if Harry was alive or dead. No one could know if their mission had been successful. The only certainty was that something had disturbed the dragons. As the boat grew closer and larger in their vision, they could see the two rowers, the two brave sailors who had volunteered. They could only see one short person. Was it Harry or Edwin? Four had gone into the dragons' lair. Three seemed to be returning. Who was missing?

As the gig made its final approach, pulley and ropes were set up with a makeshift stretcher lowered towards the water, swaying uneasily in the wind. The two sailors held the gig as steady as they could. Then Grace saw Harry was there, but crumpled in a heap. Edwin placed him on the stretcher before climbing up the side himself, followed quickly by the oarsmen as soon as they heard the Captain shout, "Abandon the gig!" Without the steadying power of the oars and with the waves whipping around it, the precarious gig with its wooden dragon, capsized and sank swiftly to the seabed. Grace did not see it. She was rushing to find Harry, forgetting all about the cold.

The Captain was giving a torrent of orders: "Weigh anchor! Set the sails! Light the braziers!"

No Captain in his right mind would light a brazier aboard a wooden ship. But these were no ordinary circumstances and they had been set as far back as possible to allow their ash to fall into the sea. They were full of Dragons' Bane and smoke quickly began to bellow from the two containers. The risk of burning from the braziers was less than the risk of burning from the dragons. As the ship set sail heading east, back towards England, the southerly wind blew the smoke towards the dragons. They were now heading from the island towards the boat, streaks of flame and smoke in the sky. Harry was still unconscious and breathing unevenly. Edwin and Grace met at the Captain's cabin where Harry had been placed on a cot. They looked at each other nervously. Eleanor had begun to tend to him. Edwin looked strangely at the other cot. The great deerhound Sophie was lying on top of it, her mouth bandaged, seeping with blood. There was no time to ask questions. He reached into Harry's jacket pocket and pulled out the uncut diamond. It was the size of a hen's egg. As he did so, he said to Eleanor. "Harry's been poisoned by the dragon. Draw the humours out of him! My place is defending the ship!"

Edwin ran up on the poop deck after collecting some tools. From the gig, he had seen the Captain holding the Sword of State, glowing green. Why the Captain had it on the poop deck, he did not know. Nor did he know why there was blood on the blade. But he needed to fit the diamond to the hilt to complete its power. As Edwin sat cross-legged with his tools and the Sword on the deck, the first of the dragons swooped low across the stern of the boat. As it did so, it breathed in the fumes of the smoke and pitched into the sea, instantly asleep. The other dragons held back, seeing what had happened. But they rose high into the sky, and then they circled ever lower and lower, gathering speed, led by the oldest, largest, angriest dragon. They sped up so much their wings changed the wind. They were whipping up a whirlwind, a mini hurricane with The Saint George in the eye of the storm.

As the dragons came close to the remaining sail, Edwin finished his work and lifted the Sword above his head. The blade grew brighter than ever and then the diamond caught the reflections of the flames spewing from the dragons' mouths. The whole ship was bathed in a deep green light.

Edwin looked up and shouted. "Ascalon is reforged! Your ancestors were banished from England in exchange for mercy. Remember that! Be banished again, from England and all the islands of England forever. Take with you your hoards of stolen treasure or the wrath of Ascalon, Albion, St George and King Harry will be upon you and you and your kind will be vanquished forever."

The dragons circled around and around, faster and faster still, so that the air was drawn out of the sails and the ship lost its way. Then the flames reflected from the diamond seemed to be drawn into the Sword's blade itself. The end of the Sword became like an electric storm in reverse, throwing green bolts of light up into the sky. Suddenly, as if a decision had been made, the dragons left and like a javelin of light, sped back to the island, before circling round the top of the volcano. One by one, they pitched down into the centre of the mountain before there was a roar and a great eruption of lava and ash into the sky. Then suddenly, the mountain collapsed in behind them and the effect was as if the lights were switched off. There was a silence and all that hung over the land was a cloud of dust. The Saint George rocked out of control before the southerly wind filled the sails again.

Grace was the first to break the silence. "What just happened? I don't understand."

Edwin replied, "I reminded the dragons of the mercy they were given by St George in exchange for their banishment from England, but when they came here, they still kept their stolen treasure. It seems that the memory of that bargain, combined with their greed for the treasure has outweighed their anger. They've gone back underground to live at the edge of hell with their hoard. We can go back to live at liberty.

"But right now, we must look after Harry, and you must tell me what's been happening since I left."

Edwin and Grace ran down to the Captain's cabin where Harry and Sophie lay injured. Eleanor looked up with tears in her eyes. "Sophie will mend well, but I don't know what's wrong with Harry. He won't wake up."

She had cut the sleeve from the tweed jacket he had been wearing. Harry's arm had swollen up so that it was larger than Edwin's huge forearms. A long scratch oozed green pus. The dragon's claw now lay limp and lifeless on the floor where it had fallen after Eleanor had drawn it from his arm.

"I need help," said Eleanor looking at Edwin, tears flooding down her cheeks. "I wish Anwen were here to help us. She'd know what to do."

Edwin looked at Harry after placing the Sword on the third cot, the one that Eloise had used, so he could watch it carefully. "The dragon's venom has been drawn into Harry's blood," he said. "It must be drawn out. Anwen uses poultices. Then it will heal."

"If the dragon's poisoned him and it's in his blood," said Eleanor thoughtfully, "perhaps the Dragons' Bane is making him sleep."

"He collapsed just after the scratch and fell into this deep sleep then," replied Edwin. "He'd smoked enough of that filthy pipe too."

"Let's use more Dragons' Bane in the poultice to draw the

poison out. Then perhaps he'll be better, but I need help. I need help from Eloise."

"Where is she?" asked Edwin.

The girls looked at him. Of course he did not know. He could not know.

"She's in the hold, secured with the other traitor, Guy of Caen," said Grace bitterly.

"He's alive then?" asked Edwin, more and more confused.

"Yes!" said Eleanor, "but let's worry about Harry first. Eloise was good with the wounded after the storm. And she saved my life. I need her help now to prepare the poultices."

Edwin looked at her carefully. "I'll get the Captain to release her, and once Harry is better, you can tell me this sorry tale. If Harry doesn't survive, I shall drop Eloise overboard myself with that Guy of Caen!"

So throughout the night, Eloise and Eleanor tended to Harry, whilst the others watched and waited. Each poultice slowly seemed to pull green pus out of the wound, until finally the swelling subsided and Harry's feverish state relaxed into a normal sleep. Sophie's dressings were changed and the cuts in her mouth treated with special herbs from Anwen's dwindling supply. Edwin stood guard with the Sword of State, which he washed and oiled carefully, but never let out of his sight.

Finally just before dawn, Harry opened his eyes and looked around at the familiar faces. He saw Edwin holding the Sword of State and he saw the diamond, the oily stone, in the hilt. He smiled. Then he licked his lips and said, "Did a dragon pooh in my mouth? It tastes disgusting. And I'm never ever going to smoke again!"

Grace and Eleanor hugged him tightly. But Harry didn't

complain, even though he winced at the pressure on his sore arm. Sophie wagged her tail so that it thumped on the other cot. Eloise was pleased, but stood shamefully in silence at the side of the room. Edwin just said, "Welcome back, Harry. Good man."

Harry was exhausted and soon fell back into a deep sleep, but it was natural sleep, not a coma induced by dragons' venom. It would take until late morning before he woke again and Edwin and Harry were told the full story.

"After you rowed around the headland," Eleanor said to Harry and Edwin, "we went to speak to Eloise about my dream. It seems that Guy of Caen, who came aboard this ship with the trust of the King, didn't go overboard in the storm, but somehow survived and went into hiding in the hold. He was badly injured, but Eloise helped nurture him back to health. Then, he stole the Sword."

"That's why she went missing so much," said Harry.

"Yes," continued Eleanor. "He came up from the hold and killed two sailors guarding the door to your cabin." Then she explained the rest.

"Of course," said Harry when she had finished. "The Prophecy warned us, *To drown the Sword not once but twice will be the traitors' game.* It must have been Eloise or Guy who were responsible before."

"I'm sure they were both on that boat," answered the Captain, who had been listening quietly now. "A confidante of the King and the Queen's maid could have combined their resources and could have engineered access to the original Sword of State."

The Captain looked at them all. "You've saved the day. All

of you. I'd be within my rights to judge Guy of Caen myself, for he's murdered two of my sailors, but the Queen's maid and this French traitor will be judged when you return to Clarendon."

Edwin muttered something about throwing both the traitors overboard right now, but Harry said quietly, "I think the Captain is right, Edwin. They must face the King's own justice."

22. Traitors' Gate

"I have a gift for you, Harry," said Edwin.

It was the middle of the night and the children and Edwin were sitting around Master John's table in the kennels at Clarendon Palace, where they had arrived little more than half an hour before.

They were all saddle sore from their journey on horseback up from Christchurch where they landed. They had said fond farewells to the Captain and his crew, before following the River Avon back up to Sarum and thence to Clarendon Palace.

One of the King's guards had accompanied them, alerted to meet them with signals, as they progressed along the south coast. Eloise and Guy of Caen had been taken separately to the dungeons in disgrace.

The sight of the big huntsman's face and his smile had been a joy to them. So had the huge bowls of soup and mead. Without Eloise to restrain them, they all had a little much, children included and became talkative and chatty. Sophie, now fully recovered, had had to run alongside them all the way and lay exhausted under the table, curled up at their feet.

Edwin got up to look in his bag, then found what he wanted and wrapped it in a cloak, before dumping it on a table. "If we had to face any other adversary, I would have lent this to you before. But against the dragons, it would have been wrong. Now you've proved your worth, so it is a gift."

"Well, what is it?" asked Grace excitedly. Like everyone, she loved presents whether they were hers or not.

"Stand up, young Harry," said Edwin, mellow, even without his pipe, which he swore he would never touch again after the experience with the Dragons' Bane. "And you girls shut your eyes. No peeping!"

Edwin took the gift from the package and, telling Harry to put his hands in the air, thrust it over his shoulders.

"You can open them now," said Edwin.

"Wow!" gasped the girls as they looked at Harry, dressed in a chainmail coat.

"It's wonderful," said Harry. "And it's so light."

Master John looked at them. "Master Edwin may make a fabulous Sword of State, but he can't make a living from that! He's known throughout the kingdom for making the lightest and finest chainmail."

"Surely," said Eleanor, slightly jealously, "chainmail is for grown-ups."

"Grown-ups," said Edwin with good cheer, "and princes and knights, but also for dwarves, the bravest of them all. This was mine when I was younger, but now it is Harry's! He's as brave as a dwarf. Almost anyway." They all laughed at that.

"How can I possibly thank you?" asked Harry.

"By wearing it with pride and honour, and living up to the bravery you've already shown. That is all."

Suddenly Grace yawned and the others found it was catching. The journey and the mead were upon them, and they were all exhausted.

"To bed with you all," said Master John. "The Queen will see you at dawn and that's only a few hours away."

As they pulled blankets over their tired bodies, sleep soon overcame them, even lying on straw mattresses set around the same room. But Eleanor lifted herself up on one arm and looked at Master John, sitting talking at the table. "What will happen to Eloise, Master John?"

"I don't know, Eleanor, but I can tell you the Queen and the King are both just. Since the Queen is the only one who can understand her sign language, we may learn more tomorrow," he replied.

It was not a good enough answer, but it would have to do and soon she too nodded off. All of them felt the beds were swaying as if they were still at sea.

It seemed to be just a moment before they were all stirred from their rest. As if by magic, the girls' cloaks had been cleaned and Harry's new chainmail had been polished, but it was not magic. Master John had fixed it with the Palace staff. "We cannot have you looking scruffy when you're presented to the Queen."

So once again, the children found themselves in the presence of Queen Eleanor, Queen of England and Duchess of Normandy and Aquitaine. This time it was no less daunting, even though the room was familiar. Sophie stood with them. Before them, on a long red velvet cushion sat the Great Sword of State. Somehow during the journey back from Hell's Bay, Edwin had managed to gild the hilt and decorate it ready for a State occasion.

"So you have fulfilled the Prophecy. There are those who say that our lives are all predetermined and this is your destiny. But from what I have been told, it's clear your destiny has been in your hands too. I congratulate you.

"You will present the Great Sword of State to the King and the Court this morning. It is not a moment too soon. Everyone is gathered."

The children stood stiffly and silently. This might almost be another torment, since meeting the King himself might be as scary as meeting the dragons.

It was Eleanor who broke the silence. She could not resist asking, "What will happen to Eloise? I don't believe she's evil!"

"Nor do I," said the Queen, an answer that surprised them. "But she's a traitor. Not once, but twice over. She must be punished."

"But Your Majesty," stuttered Eleanor.

"Silence!" said the Queen. "You will not speak again until asked.

"I have interviewed Eloise." At this moment, the Queen beckoned and they saw Eloise had been standing in the corner accompanied by a malevolent looking old woman, her prison warder. Eloise looked quite different. Her head had been completely shaved and she was dressed in a shapeless sackcloth, the garment of a prisoner. The children stood still and stared. Only Sophie moved and went towards Eloise nuzzling her, an indication of support, but Eloise stood stock-still. The Queen watched with interest before she continued.

"It seems that she's been under the compulsion of Guy of Caen and of the King of France, a curse if you like. Her brother, unknown to me, is a captive of the King of France. She had been given guarantees of his safety if she did what she was asked."

The Queen spat the next words, "I know too well what little those guarantees mean from him.

"But still, Eloise has betrayed my trust and the King's, just as Guy of Caen has betrayed the King's trust, pretending to be a loyal subject. Her fate will be at the mercy of the King."

Eleanor could not wait to speak. "But she saved my life!" The Queen looked aghast at the interruption, given she had commanded them to be silent. "And she nursed my wounds," said Harry for good measure.

The Queen softened slightly. "Well, her pride clearly prevented her from telling me that after her confession. It is in her favour, as is the fact that Sophie clearly trusts her. Her fate still lies with the King."

A curtain at the back of the room twitched. "It most certainly does," said a deep and angry voice.

The time it was the Queen's turn to show surprise, as she turned and curtsied low, bowing her head. Eloise and then the girls followed suit. Harry bowed. Here was a giant of a man, his presence unexpected. King Henry II of England himself.

"Stand," he said gruffly. "Few things have angered me more than this treachery, but then I have also heard of your heroics these last few days. That is commendable. I congratulate you."

Uncertain how to behave in front of a King, especially an angry King, the children remained silent. Even Sophie seemed to stand at attention.

"You think this Eloise deserves mercy do you?" asked the King, his eyes boring into Eleanor's.

"Y- y- yes, Sir." answered Eleanor nervously.

"And you two?" said the King turning to Harry and Grace who both nodded.

"Your sense of mercy is commendable. Since this treachery remains secret, I am able to offer mercy and Eloise won't face execution. This will be my gift of thanks and will be your reward.

"Guy of Caen deserves a far greater punishment, but in fact he will be returned to his overlord, the King of France. His safe passage will result in the freedom of Eloise's brother, who will henceforth live under my protection and in my service. This will be her reward for the kindness she showed you and her last-minute change of heart which resulted in the capture of Sir Guy. But the punishment of Eloise is this. She will never see her brother again and she'll be banished from the kingdom to remain an outlaw forever."

The King turned to the Queen, "Get the girl taken to the dungeon ready to be thrown out of the Traitors' Gate. These children must prepare for the ceremony."

The King left as swiftly as he arrived, with the Queen curtseying low again and bowing her head, all the others following suit.

When he had gone, she turned to the children. "There. You have your answer and the King's mercy too. You must prepare. Master John will show you what to do." It was clear they were dismissed.

It was an hour later. The Great West Door of Clarendon Palace was thrown open and the trumpets sounded. The children led the King and the Queen into the Great Hall of the Palace as the nobles of the court stood and cheered. Harry's arm still hurt and so the girls had to support him as he held the Sword, taller than him, and nearly as heavy, above his head. Sophie walked erect and smart beside them, after being brushed by Eleanor.

As the Sword was placed on its cushion in front of the King and Queen, seated on their thrones, the children and Sophie withdrew.

There was a sudden sense of anti-climax and disappointment. The Court's session had started and the children were no longer the centre of attention. It was Grace who voiced what they all felt: "I want to go home now. I even miss Horrible Hair Bun."

It was Master John who brought them away from the Great Hall.

"What does it mean to be banished?" asked Eleanor.

"Someone who is banished must live outside normal society. They may not mix with others and they become outlaws. It's better than death though," he answered. He might have added "only just," but he thought better of it.

"How do we get home? Edgar said we'd need to find another door," said Grace.

Master John looked sympathetically at her. "I can't answer that. I don't even know how you were brought here." He smiled at them tenderly. "But for as long as you need it, your home can be with me."

They all thanked him, but he knew their hearts were not in it, fond as he was of them.

"Can we go and see Eloise? I want to say goodbye," asked Eleanor.

"Yes. We may, if we are in time," was Master John's reply.

So Master John led them to the dungeon. As they went Harry said, "I suppose that's what was meant in the Prophecy: *Freedom and not the end lies through the traitors' gate.*"

"Banishment doesn't exactly sound like freedom," said Eleanor sadly.

"Here," said Master John, after leading them down steep stairs into the dank dungeon. "It looks like we're just in time. There's Eloise, waiting to be released into the forest through the Traitors' Gate."

They stood next to the guard, looking through the portcullis gate that had been raised. Master John looked through the gate and said, "See the beautiful day and the land beyond. You must be grateful Eloise has her freedom."

The children and Eloise looked at each other and at John strangely. They just thought he was being optimistic. All they could see was a stone corridor stretching into the distance. Sophie began acting strangely too, her ears pricked forward and sniffing the air. She was excited.

Grace suddenly understood, "It's the door to The Library! It's time for us to go home. It's not Eloise we have to say goodbye to. It's Master John."

Grace hugged John and skipped through the gate, into the corridor.

"Where's she gone?" asked John who could only see the trees and the land outside.

"She's on her way home," said Harry with sudden realisation. "We must say goodbye, John. Thank you for everything." Master John did not understand.

"Come on," shouted Grace from the other side. "You never

157

know when it might shut."

So the farewells were swift and unsatisfactory. Three children, Eloise and Sophie went through the gate and then when they turned around, there was just a blank wall.

Master John looked through the gate at the forest, bemused. He knew he would miss them all.

23. Tea with Great Uncle Jasper

Grace bounded up the stairs with Sophie close behind her. She turned into the main reading room of The Library and ran straight into her Great Uncle Jasper. Sophie licked his hand and smiled at him. Moments later, the others were around him too.

"Well, well," said Great Uncle Jasper kindly. "You're all back safely. How excellent. I didn't expect it would be quite so soon, but I should have guessed. The Library opened a door for me from my study. That doesn't happen too often."

He looked them up and down and said to the girls with a wry smile on his face, "I'm not sure nighties are quite appropriate at this time of day. And Harry, I would have thought it was a bit hot and heavy for chainmail in here. Let me help you."

Whilst Harry was helped out of his chainmail, the girls looked down at themselves and saw their beautiful purple robes had vanished and they were back in their bedtime clothes. The robes had been pulled back into the books without them noticing.

"But now," added Great Uncle Jasper. "We're being rude. You must introduce me to your friend."

"This is Eloise," said Harry. Jasper held his hand out. She curtsied and was quite uncertain what to do. But he told her to stand up and he shook her hand, quietly smiling and saying, "Welcome to The Palace Library."

"Eloise can't talk," added Harry, "but she's sweet. And wise."

"Well Edgar is a good talker," said Jasper, "and I'm sure he'll be happy to have a companion here. It must get lonely sometimes, even with Sophie."

"You mean Eloise will stay here in The Library?" asked Eleanor.

"Well I think she'll have to," said Great Uncle Jasper knowingly. "She can't exactly go back to Clarendon Palace can she? And I doubt The Library will let her home with us."

Eloise looked a little bemused by this all, but Grace had other things on her mind. "Do you think Edgar has any chocolate cake?" she asked.

"Mmmm. I'm not sure. I have to tell you Edgar isn't quite himself at the moment."

"Is he ill?" asked Grace, worried suddenly.

"Oh no. It's just that he's never seen a television before and he's quite engrossed. Although he works for The Witan, he's quite the monarchist and obviously he couldn't be at the last Diamond Jubilee in person. Queen Victoria made him a Privy Councillor you know. That's where he got that lovely blue coat from. I'm quite jealous really.

"Anyway, I think we're just in time. Come and watch. It's all about to start."

"What's about to start?" asked Grace.

"It's the service in St Paul's for Queen Elizabeth's Diamond Jubilee," replied Edgar. "I think you'll like it."

Inwardly the children groaned. A church service was boring, but they were too polite to say.

Edgar was engrossed in the screen. He gave a little wave and an indication to be quiet, quite forgetting his manners. Then they all sat down together.

The service was about to start and they saw Queen Elizabeth II step out of her carriage with Prince Phillip and move up the cathedral steps.

"I think you'll like this bit," said Great Uncle Jasper encouragingly. "Watch carefully."

Then they understood what he meant, for there on the television screen they saw the Lord Mayor of London lead the Queen into the cathedral for the service. Raised in his hands was the Sword of State. It seemed like only that morning that they had been doing the very same thing.

It was only that morning, but another time and another place.

If you enjoyed The Palace Library, be the first to hear about sequels and new releases!

Ask your parents to sign up to my no-spam mailing list at:

thepalacelibrary.com

The sequel,

Guardians of The Scroll,

will be published in December 2015

Read sample chapters on the following pages.

Read sample chapters from the sequel:

Guardians of The Scroll

1.

A screech. A thump. The cracking of glass.

Harry was falling in darkness, blind. He couldn't breathe. He tried to thrash around. He couldn't move. He tried to scream. He couldn't make a sound.

Tap-tap-tap. Tap-tap-tap. Tap-tap-tap.

Harry realised that he was locked in a nightmare. But the tapping wasn't in his dream. It was real, repeating like an alarm clock, battling to wake him.

Harry opened his eyes. He wasn't blind after all, but all he saw was a dragon's claw in his arm, shrouded in smoke. He heard himself scream. The ground was rushing towards him and he was going to be crushed. No. It was water below, dark and murky, waiting to swallow him. He was going to drown. With a desperate struggle, he turned his head and managed to breathe a proper mouthful of air.

His face was in his pillow and his hands were spread out either side of him like a sky diver. He could move them. He scratched the scar on his arm. It was throbbing gently, but not agony. "It's still just a scar," he said out loud. Hearing the sound of his own voice calmed him. The faint glimmer of light through the curtains felt different to the darkness before. Yes, now he really was awake.

Tap-tap-tap. Tap-tap-tap.

Something was knocking at the window. This was real, not part of the dream. Harry got out of bed, pulling a thin blanket around him to keep warm.

The heavy curtains scraped noisily across the old brass rail as he drew them open. His room looked across the garden towards the great cedar tree and the ha-ha. The windows of the old house were lead-paned in diamond patterns. One pane was broken and ice had drawn feathers of frozen condensation on the inside. No wonder Harry was so cold. Crystals gathered under his fingernails as he scraped frost off the window to see out. Suddenly he jumped and goosebumps crawled up his arms. The beak of a bird thrust forward, tapping at the glass.

Tap-tap-tap. Tap-tap-tap.

Harry fumbled at the latch of the window, stiff with age and ice. He gave it a thump and it suddenly jerked wide open. The bird fell off the windowsill.

"Hell!" muttered Harry to himself. The bird spun and tumbled before recovering near the ground. It swooped back across the roof of the house. "At least, it's not hurt," thought

Harry as he saw it fly. Its feathers were the colour of tarnished brass. He had the strange feeling that it was trying to tell him something.

Clouds high in the sky drifted across the winter moon as it struggled to light up the garden. A gap in the clouds allowed Harry to see the old cedar tree clearly. To his surprise, he noticed two people standing in its shadow, backs towards him. One was tall, thin, a dark grey hoody covering his head. The other was shorter, stout, with a long old-fashioned cloak draped over his shoulders. The night was still, so Harry could just about hear what they were saying.

"You're sure this is the genuine thing?" said the tall person - definitely a man - flicking through pages of paper.

"There's no doubt. It's the most precious artefact in The Palace Library. It's rare, unique probably." The high-pitched voice trembled: "Is it valuable?"

"Yesss," hissed the tall man, drawing his fingers across the pages to feel them as much as read them.

"Then you'll pay me what you said?" asked the other. "Perhaps I should ask for more?" The voice cracked.

Harry stared in disbelief as the tall man moved his hand from the sheaf of papers to the neck of the shorter person and squeezed it tight. "More? More? This was taken from my family a long, long time ago. You ought to have nothing at all." The hand moved away from the short man's neck and he condescended to say, "You shall have what I agreed. That is all."

Harry started to cry out "Stop!" Some instinct held him back, but not before the 's' echoed round the garden like a hiss. The taller man turned and looked up. Their eyes met for a moment that felt like minutes. Harry threw himself below the window. He was sure the sound of his heart thumping on the floorboards would be heard all over the house. Harry knew the tall man had seen him. He could still hear the strangers as he lay flat on the bedroom floor, as frozen with fear as he had been in his nightmare.

"Who was that?" demanded the tall man.

"It's just a boy," said the other. "Harry. He often comes to stay here. Don't worry about him."

"Harry? You're sure?"

"Yes. I told you, he comes to stay with his sister, Eleanor. They're just children."

"Don't tell me they have another friend? Grace?" He spat the name out like a bad taste in the mouth.

"Yes, but how do you know?" answered the short one.

"They are trouble."

If Harry had been able to see them, he would have seen the thin hand strike again and squeeze until the other was on his knees. "You will not be paid until they are dealt with. You'll hear from me again soon. Now go. GO!"

Harry heard someone panting and running. And although Harry had not seen the assault, he felt their fear. The short fat person would have seen the same face and be terrified, as Harry was terrified. The tall man had a pale gaunt face, skin taut across the bones, ancient, like the fingers. But it was the eyes that were frightening. Harry had never seen eyes like that. They were demonic. They looked like cat's eyes, alive with orange fire. The pupils were single black needles, filled with hate.

2.

Harry cowered on the floor for several minutes before he dared to lift his head. His teeth were chattering. The blanket had fallen from his shoulders and lay crumpled on the floor. Cold air poured in through the open window and wrapped around him, but he was already frozen with fear. He had to shut the window. Now. Without being seen. He stretched out his arm and pulled the metal frame tight and twitched the heavy curtains together. The wound from the dragon's claw ached, even though it had fully healed months before. He rubbed the scar, a habit that had formed without him noticing. He had to get warm. He looked around and spotted a box of matches on the mantelpiece.

Harry wasn't sure if he was allowed to light the fire, but he was so cold he didn't care if he got into trouble with Horrible Hair Bun, Great Uncle Jasper's witch of a housekeeper. He needed to warm up and think. He struck the first match, but the matches were damp and the head just withered away into nothing, dropping a tiny, glowing spark on the hearth where a pile of twigs, wood and bark lay ready. The next two matches were the same. Harry took three matches at once, holding them at arm's length, and struck them together towards the centre of the fireplace.

One of the match heads flew back at him. "Damn and blast," he muttered as it burnt the skin on his hand, making him drop the box. Sucking the burn, he threw the spent matches into the centre of the pile of twigs. The glow of the match heads faded into nothing, but a tiny column of smoke began to rise upwards. There was a rustling, and a trickle of dust began to fall down the chimney, followed by chunks of soot mixed with more twigs and moss. Something was bumping around in the chimney. Harry crouched and tried to look up, but leapt back quickly as dust dropped into his eyes. A bird fell with a thump into the centre of the twigs. It flapped a couple of times, coughed and spluttered. It was covered in soot and dirt. So was Harry's face, he could feel grit on his eyeballs.

The bird's eyes were shut. It flapped once or twice more, and then was still. Harry stepped forward, blinking and rubbing his eyes, forgetting the cold. As he bent towards the hearth, he realised it was the same bird that had tapped on the window, but it was smaller and withered, grey rather than the colour of tarnished bronze. He thought he should pick it up and take it to Eleanor, who knew what to do with injured animals. Then, as he bent down to pick the bird up, the twigs in the fire burst into flame, as if they were the head of an enormous match, and the whole pile began to burn furiously.

Instinctively Harry stepped back, and tripped over the edge of a carpet. "Ow!" he yelped as his bottom hit the wooden floor with a thump. The flames engulfed the bird and everything else in the fireplace. Harry wondered how he could help it, looking desperately around for some sort of tool to reach into the fire, but there was nothing.

Sickened that he could do nothing, Harry stared as the fire grew stronger. At first, it was a deep, golden colour, and then, even though the twigs were burned to ash, there was still a fierce green flame. Harry saw something moving within the fire. Was the bird that had come down the chimney still alive? It was! But he couldn't get close. "What can I do?" he shouted in frustration. From green, the flames turned to blue, and then to orange. Suddenly the creature stood up, wings outstretched, fanning the last of the fire into a massive conflagration. It looked as if it was bathing in the flames.

This wasn't the small frail bird that Harry had seen. This was much bigger. This bird was pure, brilliant white with a wingspan that touched the sides of the chimney breast.

Harry suddenly thought of the blanket. He could wrap it around the bird and smother the flames. However, when he turned back from picking it up, it was too late. The bird's wings were moving so quickly that Harry lost sight of their shape, and their draught extinguished the flames. All that was left of the fire was burning in the bird's tail-feathers. Piercing sapphire-blue eyes stared at Harry, and he felt that he was staring at a person. Then the bird lifted its wings and flew from the fireplace. The last remnants of flame streamed from its tail feathers in all the colours Harry had seen: red, green, purple, blue and orange. A trail of smoke followed the bird and filled the room. It flew around the bed twice, sat on the mantelpiece, folded its wings and preened itself. The fire in the hearth was gone, and the fire on the bird's tail was gone. The room was dark.

Sleeve across his face, spluttering from the smoke, Harry opened the window, trying not to show himself to anyone outside. The bird flew past Harry's head so closely it brushed against his hair and then went straight up into the sky.

Crouching low, Harry saw it circle and swoop around the top of the cedar tree. He dared to raise his head and look around carefully. There was no sign of the people he had seen before, or the terrible eyes. The bird was hovering with its wings outstretched. Harry was sure he heard the bird say, "Thank you."

But he put the thought aside because, of course, birds don't speak.

3.

Harry's mind was racing as fast as his teeth were chattering. What on earth was the bird? What were those two people doing in the middle of the night in Great Uncle Jasper's garden? Was this the beginning of some new adventure? Someone had been stealing something, and one of the thieves was hardly normal – hardly human. "Have to get warm to think," he said to himself. Pulling open a drawer, he dragged two jumpers over his pyjamas, rummaged in a cupboard and put a jacket on top. Then he nearly fell over pulling on a pair of trousers, the pyjamas beneath sticking out ridiculously.

The twigs in the fireplace had burnt so fiercely that nothing remained in the hearth but the tiniest trace of white ash. Looking around, Harry realised that there weren't any logs in the room, so he wouldn't have got far with lighting a fire anyway. Having his clothes on made him just a bit warmer. He decided to get back into bed, but not before grabbing an old cap and a scarf off the back of the door.

Still shivering under the bedclothes, he heard the grandfather clock at the end of the long corridor strike the hour. Only four o'clock! He was desperate to speak to his sister Eleanor and his cousin Grace but there was no way he could creep along the squeaky corridor without waking Horrible Hair Bun. When he had last done that he had been locked in his room for a whole day with nothing to do. He sighed in frustration. It was all too unreal and a reminder of the events last summer that had started here in this big house and The Palace Library.

With these thoughts winding around and around in his head, Harry decided to wait until he heard the six o'clock chimes. He might get away without too much grief from Horrible Hair Bun then. Minutes passed like hours as he heard the quarters and the hours strike. There was no chance of sleep with so much to think about. But then, once he had warmed up a little, Harry did exactly that.

When he woke, daylight was seeping through the curtains and Harry felt much better, though still not very warm. He was glad he was fully clothed, otherwise he might have thought the whole thing was just part of his nightmare.

He leapt out of bed and ran down the corridor. The grandfather clock's hands stood at twenty-eight minutes past eight. Help! Breakfast was at half-past. Horrible Hair Bun always insisted that they were all at the table by then, otherwise they would go without. Harry pelted down two flights of stairs to join the others in the kitchen and sat in his place just as the clock chimed the half-hour. Horrible Hair Bun scowled at him as she set down a plate of eggs and bacon. Whatever else was wrong with her, her cooking was good.

"I'm so sorry. I nearly overslept," he said politely. It made no difference to her scowl.

"Take your cap off. It's ridiculous to wear it inside." When Harry did so, she scowled again, "Wash your face properly after breakfast."

"Just in time, Harry," said Eleanor, winking at him.

"How do you wink like that?" asked Grace, scrunching her eyes in an unsuccessful attempt to copy her elder cousin. Then she saw Harry and giggled. "What are you wearing? You look like a fat scarecrow!"

"Never mind. I need to talk to you both," whispered Harry.

He gobbled his food, barely chewing the bacon. He couldn't wait till Horrible Hair Bun left the kitchen. She always went to check their rooms, eager to scold the children if they were too untidy. Harry hadn't made his bed, so he knew he'd be in trouble, but he was more anxious to tell the girls about the bird, the fire and the strangers. As soon as Hair Bun had left the room, he started talking excitedly.

"Slow down Harry!" said Eleanor. "You look as if you're about to explode. And finish chewing first! You're spraying toast crumbs all over me. It's disgusting."

Harry gulped so quickly at a glass of water that some of it dribbled down his jumper. "This is serious," he began.

As he finished telling his story Grace looked at him out of her clear blue eyes and said, "Are you sure you didn't set the little bird on fire, Harry?"

"Of course I wouldn't have set the bird on fire! I didn't even know it was there. And anyway, I barely managed to get a spark off the matches, let alone set the twigs on fire."

"There's a boy at school who does horrible things to animals," said Grace. Harry frowned and Grace suddenly realised that it sounded like an accusation. "But I know you're not like that. I was just checking."

"You mean the fire just started by itself?" asked Eleanor.

"I know it sounds strange," said Harry, still cross from Grace's accusation but having the sense to ignore it. "The fire just erupted on its own. The matches wouldn't work. And anyway I've never seen a fire that burned so quickly or fiercely."

"I wish I'd been there to see it," said Eleanor. "The thing I don't understand is why the bird was white." Harry was about to ask why did that matter, when he realised what he had missed. Stupid! he thought. Maybe the cold had got to his brain in the night.

"I thought they were..." said Eleanor, but Harry interrupted, "It's a Phoenix. Of course."

"Durr," said Eleanor. "Of course it's a Phoenix. It was being reborn in your fireplace and you didn't even realise? Durr."

Grace, who hadn't realised either, decided not to own up but changed the subject instead, "What about the people? Who were they?"

"The tall man - if he was human at all - I'm sure I've never seen before."

"Then how did he know you?" said Grace.

"I dunno. It's weird."

But then there came the familiar screech of Horrible Hair Bun in a temper.

"Here it comes. We're in trouble now," said Harry.

"You're in trouble, you mean," replied Eleanor.

Horrible Hair Bun threw open the door and looked at Harry, finger pointing. He froze, bracing himself against the torrent of words he was expecting about not making his bed. But they didn't come at first. As Harry and the girls looked at Horrible Hair Bun, they saw her draw her breath in, before bellowing in a louder scream than ever before, "Harry Godwinson. I have to say, I never expected it of you, especially at your age. I will not have you smoking in this house - or at all."

Harry looked up. "I wasn't smoking!"

"Don't try to deny it!" screeched the housekeeper. "I can smell the smoke quite clearly in your room. And you've broken a window."

"Harry wouldn't smoke," interrupted Eleanor. "Not after his experience last summer. He's telling the truth!"

"'His experience last summer?' You mean to say that Harry has been smoking before? It sounds as if he wasn't punished enough."

"That's not what I meant," said Eleanor, twisting a loose strand of hair, realising she had made things even worse.

"Well, Harry," asked Horrible Hair Bun. "Did you smoke last summer?"

He stammered, "It … It's a long story, and it's not really mine to tell."

"A simple yes or no will do."

"Well, yes. But I had to."

"That's absurd," said the housekeeper.

This time Grace spoke out, "You're not being fair! Harry was just trying to light the fire in his bedroom. Can't you see he's frozen? And then the matches didn't work. He couldn't even light the kindling wood. He told us."

Horrible Hair Bun was silent for a moment, but only a moment. "I've had enough of you covering up for Harry. There hasn't been a fire laid in that fireplace in my lifetime.

The chimney has always been blocked up. Aha, I've caught you out, haven't I? I'm going to take you to see your Great Uncle Jasper right now. He will know what to do with you and he will decide how to punish you, Harry, for smoking and all of you for lying. I expect he will beat you."

4.

Horrible Hair Bun frogmarched the children across bare oak floorboards to Great Uncle Jasper's study. Ancient portraits of men wearing beards and old-fashioned clothes looked down at them sternly as she knocked at the door.

"Enter."

Horrible Hair Bun threw open the door. A pile of well-read books wobbled and then settled back into organised chaos. Warmth and cosiness wafted out of the room before the children even stepped inside. A fire crackled between two huge sets of bookshelves. Strange artefacts with unknown uses filled gaps in various places on the shelves.

"Are you cold, Harry?" asked Great Uncle Jasper from behind a big mahogany and leather desk. For the first time that morning, Harry became self-conscious about what he was wearing. He still had his school scarf wrapped around his neck and was holding the old tweed cap in his hand.

Before Harry had a chance to answer, Great Uncle Jasper

asked, "Which room is Harry sleeping in?"

"The green room in the West Wing," Horrible Hair Bun said.

"I think we'd better move him. The fireplace doesn't work there and the chimney is blocked up. It must be terribly cold with all this frost. I'll keep the children here for the moment until Harry has warmed up."

"I've brought them here for punishment."

"Oh?" Great Uncle Jasper's eyebrows lifted high up his forehead.

"Harry has been smoking and these others covering up for him."

"Has he indeed?" The eyebrows dropped into a frown.

"In his bedroom."

"That sounds most unwise. Stupid even - so easily discovered. Leave the children here now. I'll deal with it. I've some other things to discuss with them as it happens." He looked at the children with a stern face before turning back to the housekeeper. "Perhaps you could organise Harry's bedroom now?"

Horrible Hair Bun looked disappointed, as if she didn't want to miss out on any punishment the children might be getting. "Shall I wait here in case you need me, sir?"

"No, thank you, Mrs. Higgsbottom. I will look after this myself."

After the housekeeper left the room Great Uncle Jasper pulled open a drawer of his desk and took out a small brown package wrapped with string. He put it down in front of him, tapping it with his fingers.

"Sit down, children. Sit down."

The girls sat on the cushioned fender in front of the fire, but Harry, beginning to overheat in so many layers, sank into the little armchair opposite the desk. Great Uncle Jasper knew, of course, about Harry's adventures the previous summer, which the housekeeper did not. He frowned and for a moment Harry became worried. Great Uncle Jasper was a kind man, but none of the children knew him that well. He was just a little distant, even though Harry and Eleanor sometimes came to his big country house on holiday when their parents were working, usually when they could see their orphaned cousin Grace.

He looked at Harry and said, "It would surprise me if you had been smoking after your experience at Hell's Bay last summer Harry. Were you?"

"No, sir."

"Well that's that, then," said Great Uncle Jasper.

"You believe me?" asked Harry.

"Of course. You don't strike me as the lying type. None of you do," he added, looking at the girls.

Then Harry asked, "But I don't understand how the bird could have fallen down the chimney if the fireplace is blocked up. All I was trying to do was set light to all the twigs in the hearth."

Great Uncle Jasper raised his eyebrows again. "I think you had better explain more about the bird. Make yourself comfortable and tell me your story. Perhaps you might start from the beginning - always a good plan." His eyes twinkled as he added, "After all, Mrs Higgsbottom might never forgive me if I didn't ask you. She does become stricter with time." So Harry told his tale for the second time that morning. As he talked, from time to time Great Uncle Jasper tapped his fingers on the little parcel, especially when he heard about the stranger with the fiery eyes. When he had finished, Great Uncle Jasper said, "You're sure both these people knew about you, but you couldn't recognise them."

"Yes. Quite sure. They were too far away. But those eyes. I'll never forget them. They were horrid - demonic. The other funny thing is that the bird was trying to tell me something, some message, but I just don't know what. He wasn't talking exactly. I know it sounds silly, but it was more like a voice in my head, in a language I couldn't understand."

"That is odd," said Grace. "Maybe it's a bit like Sophie, and her empathy."

"Yes," Eleanor added, "And I bet Sophie thinks so too. Don't you, Sophie?" She turned to the noble deerhound lying on the Persian carpet in front of the fireplace. While Harry was telling his story, Sophie had silently crept up and pushed her nose into Eleanor's hand. Eleanor was stroking her.

"Well, well," said Great Uncle Jasper. "That's another surprise this morning, but at least it's not an unpleasant surprise. Tell me, Eleanor, where did Sophie come from?"

"Wh - what do you mean?" replied Eleanor, nervously, as if she'd done something wrong. "She was just here all of sudden. I supposed she'd been here all along."

"No," said Great Uncle Jasper. "Don't you recall? Sophie lives in The Palace Library. She shouldn't be here at all. She should be with Edgar and Eloise. This can mean only one thing. The Palace Library and this house must have become magically linked again."

"So that's how the Phoenix came to fall down the chimney," said Grace.

"Perhaps," said Great Uncle Jasper, deep in thought. "Without doubt you have seen the rebirth of a Phoenix. You are privileged. Very few people in the whole history of the world have seen it. There is only one Phoenix and he is reborn in fire every few hundred years. No one knows when it will happen. I have never heard of the Phoenix ever being any colour other than gold, except in heraldry and there's a connection with The Palace Library there too. This is curious."

"I suppose it was a bit gold when I first saw it at the window and falling down the chimney, but it was so sooty. When it came back to life it was definitely white," said Harry, still too shaken by the whole experience to really consider it a privilege.

Just then a voice boomed through the wall behind Great Uncle Jasper, and said, "It's not quite right that the Phoenix is always gold, but another colour is very unusual. A White Phoenix is recorded in Plutarch's Life of Caesar. That's apart from the one on the Council of the Book's heraldic shield. Could you give me a hand, do you think?"

"Edgar!" shouted the children happily, recognising the voice.

Behind Jasper, one of the piles of books on the floor had begun swaying from side to side. The top few books slipped off the stack and hit the floor. A large and heavy bookcase nearby began to wobble.

"I think something's blocking the door," shouted Edgar. The bookcase began to wobble more dangerously.

"Wait!" commanded Great Uncle Jasper. "Girls, clear these books out of the way. Quickly. Harry, help me move the bookcase."

Harry and Great Uncle Jasper both grunted as they pushed

the heavy bookcase. Behind it was a simple wooden door without a handle.

"Try now, Edgar."

"That's better," said the voice on the other side and a moment later the elderly man, who had befriended the children the year before, stood before them, unchanged with his silver-grey beard and deep blue tail-coat covered with gold brocade. As he tried to stand up straight, the children mobbed him. He mustered all the dignity he could to greet Great Uncle Jasper with formality, "Good morning, Sir."

"Good morning, Edgar."

Edgar said, "I think you'd better come in. When Sophie vanished and the magical door appeared, we hoped we might see you. Eloise has gone to make some hot chocolate. The food's improved no end since she's taken an interest in the cookery section. The hot chocolate's from a Belgian book, I think. They're masters of chocolate you know, the Belgians."

The children looked round at their Great Uncle. "Go on," he said kindly. "That's an offer we can't refuse. Once we're in the Library, we can try and get to the bottom of these thieves - as that is what they must be - and of The Phoenix."

"Just watch out," said Edgar, "This door has appeared in a most unusual place. The geography of the place is all muddled up."

5.

Sophie leapt through the door, but the last thing she expected was a highly polished mahogany table on the other side, slippery as ice. She did the splits with her front feet and her nose whacked the table. Her hind paws had no better grip and she slid over the edge on her tummy, tumbling to the floor with a yelp.

"Sophie!" cried Eleanor, nearly falling herself in her anxiety for the dog, but by the time she was through the door Sophie had picked herself up. She shook herself and stood elegant once more, smiling in her own way.

"It's a map table," announced Edgar, making his way much more gingerly. "I really don't know what right a door has to be on top of a map table. A door should be in a wall."

Grace walked cautiously to the edge. Then she saw Eloise beneath her, holding her arms up ready to catch her. The intention was clear but Eloise said nothing. She couldn't. She was mute. With a huge smile Grace launched herself into her arms.

Eloise's long dark hair was tied back in a plait and she wore a plain dress. She looked completely different from the forlorn prisoner she had been at the end of their adventures the previous summer. At that time she had had a shaved head and had been dressed in rags. Now even the scar that disfigured half her face seemed to have faded as she smiled in obvious pleasure at seeing them all.

A set of library ladders stood at the edge of the table and Edgar climbed down. Harry turned back to look into Great Uncle Jasper's study and stared at the mess of books on the floor. "I think Mrs Higgsbottom will have something to say about this when she sees it. I do hope she won't blame you, Harry," said Great Uncle Jasper. "Carry on. I'll join you in a moment."

Harry jumped down from the table and Great Uncle Jasper turned back into his study. He collected the small brown package wrapped with string and slipped it into his pocket. As his foot touched the floor of The Palace Library, there was a loud bang. The door slammed shut. The whole quivering frame now sank into the table, which began to shake like a jelly. Within seconds, it vanished without trace.

As if all this had been the most normal thing in the world, Great Uncle Jasper said politely, "Good morning, Eloise." She curtsied to him and nodded her head. Then she turned to the children and indicated the hot chocolate waiting for them.

The grown-ups had small, delicate porcelain cups, with a swirl of dark chocolate inside them. The children had steaming mugs with a milky frothy top. Harry saw dragons flying round and round in circles on his mug. Grace's was dark blue with twinkling stars. One of the deerhounds running around Eleanor's mug was just like Sophie.

"Can I have some marshmallows please?" asked Grace with her most angelic smile. Eloise frowned.

"She doesn't know what marshmallows are," said Edgar. Eloise had come to the Library from her own time of 1164 and still had a lot of catching up to do. "They're a sort of sweet, Eloise. You should find a book on the second shelf behind you."

Eloise found the book, turned to the page on marshmallows and showed Grace the picture. "Yes please!" said Grace. So Eloise tipped the book and the marshmallows fell right off the page into the cup. "Wow! Thank you."

While all three of them had a portion of marshmallows Great Uncle Jasper told Eloise and Edgar about the Phoenix and the strange people stealing something.

"I think this morning's events justify these three knowing more, don't you Edgar?" said Great Uncle Jasper. "More to the point, I think they need to know now, without further reference to the Council."

"Well, that was my advice to the Council last year, but it was not taken," replied Edgar a little pointedly.

"I know, Edgar and you know I agree with you."

"Non maior sed sanior," muttered Edgar.

"Come on, Edgar, you know the Council takes a vote. We can't overrule it just because we think we're in the right. That's the route to dictatorship and what we strive to avoid. I may be head of the Council, but I cannot ride roughshod over what everyone thinks."

"I know, I know."

"What does it mean?" asked Harry. "It's Latin, isn't it?"

"It means 'Not the most, but the wisest,'" said Great Uncle Jasper. "Dictators use the principle to overthrow a majority vote - and freedom. A principle of 'I know best', if you like. Anyway, it's time to share more about the Council. In the circumstances, could you find a copy of the heraldic arms of the council, please Edgar? Do you agree?"

"I agree."

"In fact, I think it's time they saw Katherine's book."

Edgar hesitated. He thought for a moment or two, then said, "Yes. I agree with that too. Democracy in action, you see." He smiled at Jasper. "I won't be long."

Edgar tottered off to find the book. When he returned, his face had not just gone white, but ashen grey. He put down a large leather-bound volume on the map table as if it were a great burden, then staggered and held onto the table with both hands, breathing hard. "It's gone, vandalised, stolen. We have failed!"

He slumped, and might have collapsed if Great Uncle Jasper had not caught him. Edgar stood up more firmly and flung open the leather book. His gnarled hands took a chunk of pages from within and flung them into the air. They settled like leaves on the floor around him. "Look. There's nothing but blanks in the binding. It's been taken. Cut and vandalised! Stolen! Replaced with blanks! On our watch!" The demonstration was his last effort. As he finally collapsed into a chair, with his head in his hands, he said, "I have failed," over and over again. Then he looked up at Jasper, pulling himself together, and said, "The Council must be called at once. This is the most serious thing since the fire."

186

Jasper nodded. He looked pale and shocked, but unlike Edgar, he was not panicking.

"What's missing? What fire?" asked Eleanor.

"The book was damaged in the Great Fire of London in 1667, but that's another story. Before that, it was in its original form - a scroll. Only after the damage from the fire was it bound up in a book."

"Maybe that's what I saw being stolen. There were certainly papers." said Harry.

Great Uncle Jasper sat down and took a deep breath. "We cannot know for sure, but yes, I think you're right. We must do whatever we can - whatever - to recover it."

"How old is it exactly?"

"We don't actually know." Jasper paused, grasping the remains of the book in his hands. "Very soon, we must convene the Council of the Book, the group which for hundreds, even thousands of years, has protected it. But you need to know more. Without doubt, you are heavily involved in this, more so perhaps than even we ever imagined." Edgar was nodding, silent. The hot chocolate was forgotten.

Great Uncle Jasper opened the vandalised volume. Only the title page remained. It was a brightly illustrated picture of a coat of arms, but instead of a conventional shield, it was shaped like a gold-coloured book and at the centre was a large white bird.

"That's it!" said Harry. "That's the exact bird I saw this morning!"

"And this," said Jasper, "is the symbol of the Council of the Book. It was drawn when the book was rebound after the fire, but the symbol of the white Phoenix is important and his actual arrival just now … well, can it really be a coincidence? The missing pages are important too. They're the pages we've come to know as Katherine's Book."

"So who was Katherine?" asked Grace.

"Katherine was a member of the Council of the Book at the time of King Arthur, but from the little we know, she was old, possibly mad, and shunned by the Court. Merlin believed what she said, however, and persuaded King Arthur to take her under his protection."

"But aren't King Arthur and Merlin just stories?" asked Grace.

"Like we thought dragons were just stories until last summer?" said Harry, rubbing the wound on his arm.

"Exactly, Harry." said Jasper.

"And the scroll, the book thingy?" asked Eleanor. "What can be so important about one book? Is it just because it's old?"

"No, no. Not just that. In the wrong hands, that book is one of the most dangerous things in the world."

"More dangerous than bombs and missiles?" asked Grace.

"Much more dangerous," replied Great Uncle Jasper. "The scroll is just one part of a much larger scroll. Katherine told Merlin and Arthur that, combined with the other parts, it could be used to wake, control or destroy all the powerful creatures of The Nether World, the creatures - or monsters – who lurk under the surface of our world. It can be used for both good and evil, which is why it must be protected."

"The Council of the Book is sworn to protect this book and look after it. We have failed," Edgar added dismally.

"Then we need to recover it," said Harry. He thought back

to the previous summer when the children had been sent to fight dragons in the past. Was this happening again?

"Let me tell you more," continued Jasper.

"Wait! Hush!" said Grace.

Jasper looked quite startled to be interrupted like this by Grace, but he listened for a moment.

Tap-tap-tap. Tap-tap-tap.

"That's what I heard in my nightmare, but it turned out real," said Harry.

Tap-tap-tap. Tap-tap-tap.

"It's the Phoenix. He wants to come in. He's at the window on the gallery by the dome." Grace stood up and pointed. "He's got a message to give us."

"How do you know?"

"I just know. And I know it's urgent." Without another word, she ran to the stairs and began to climb them two at a time.